"It's not an engagement ring,"

Nick assured her. "But when people ask to see your ring, you can show it to them."

Olivia shook her head in disbelief. "If this is not an engagement ring, then what is it?"

Nick paused a half beat. She'd taken him off guard. "This is a friendship ring," he told her. "It's a gift, and I would want you to wear it all the time. Even after the thirty days are up, and we're not pretending to be engaged anymore."

Olivia blinked at him, then shook her head and smiled. "Thank you, Nick," she said softly. "I want to be your friend forever."

As she wrapped her arms around him, Olivia felt rattled by her thoughts. Yes, they were friends. But they were also lovers. How had this gotten so complicated? And what was going to happen to her heart when her thirty days were done?

Dear Reader,

Hectic life? Too much to do, too little time? Well, Silhouette Desire provides you with the perfect emotional getaway with this month's moving stories of men and women finding love and passion. So relax, pick up a Desire novel and let yourself escape, with six wonderful, involving, totally absorbing romances.

Ultratalented author Mary Lynn Baxter kicks off November with her sultry Western style in *Slow Talkin' Texan,* the story of a MAN OF THE MONTH whose strong desires collide with an independent lady—she's silk to his denim, lace to his leather... and doing all she can to resist this *irresistible* tycoon. A small-town lawman who rescues a "lost" beauty might just find his own Christmas bride in Jennifer Greene's heartwarming *Her Holiday Secret.* Ladies, watch closely as a *Thirty-Day Fiancé* is transformed into a forever husband in Leanne Banks's third book in THE RULEBREAKERS miniseries.

Don't dare miss the intensity of an innocent wife trying to seduce her honor-bound husband in *The Oldest Living Married Virgin,* the latest in Maureen Child's spectacular miniseries THE BACHELOR BATTALION. And when a gorgeous ex-marine shows up at his old flame's ranch to round up the "wife who got away," he discovers a daughter he never knew in *The Re-Enlisted Groom* by Amy J. Fetzer. *The Forbidden Bride-to-Be* may be off-limits...but isn't that what makes the beautiful heroine in Kathryn Taylor's scandal-filled novel all the more tempting?

This November, Silhouette Desire is the place to live, love and lose yourself...to sensual romance. Enjoy!

Warm regards,

Joan Marlow Golan
Senior Editor, Silhouette Desire

Please address questions and book requests to:
Silhouette Reader Service
U.S.: 3010 Walden Ave., P.O. Box 1325, Buffalo, NY 14269
Canadian: P.O. Box 609, Fort Erie, Ont. L2A 5X3

THIRTY-DAY FIANCÉ
LEANNE BANKS

SILHOUETTE *Desire*

Published by Silhouette Books

America's Publisher of Contemporary Romance

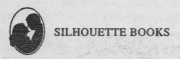

SILHOUETTE BOOKS

ISBN 0-373-76179-1

THIRTY-DAY FIANCÉ

This edition published by arrangement with Harlequin Books S.A.

® and TM are trademarks of Harlequin Books S.A., used under license. Trademarks indicated with ® are registered in the United States Patent and Trademark Office, the Canadian Trade Marks Office and in other countries.

Printed in U.S.A.

Books by Leanne Banks

Silhouette Desire

‡*Ridge: The Avenger* #987
**The Five-Minute Bride* #1058
**The Troublemaker Bride* #1070
**The You-Can't-Make-Me Bride* #1082
†*Millionaire Dad* #1166
†*The Lone Rider Takes a Bride* #1172
†*Thirty-Day Fiancé* #1179

‡   Sons and Lovers
*   How To Catch a Princess
†   The Rulebreakers

Silhouette Special Edition

A Date with Dr. Frankenstein #983
Expectant Father #1028

LEANNE BANKS

is a national number-one bestselling author of romance.
She lives in her native Virginia with her husband and son
and daughter. Recognized for both her sensual and
humorous writing with two Career Achievement Awards
from *Romantic Times Magazine,* Leanne likes creating a
story with a few grins, a generous kick of sensuality and
characters who hang around after the book is finished.
Leanne believes romance readers are the best readers in
the world because they understand that love is the greatest miracle of all. You can write to her at P.O. Box 1442,
Midlothian, VA 23113. An SASE for a reply would be
greatly appreciated.

Special acknowledgment to Neesa Hart for friendship
and tales of beheaded Barbies.

This book is dedicated to all who've been told
they're not smart enough or good enough,
yet still show us how to fly.

Prologue

More than anything, eleven-year-old Nick Nolan wanted muscles.

He wanted to be so tall and strong, the bullies wouldn't even *think* of beating on him. No matter how many hamburgers, French fries, and milk shakes he ate, Nick knew he was the scrawniest guy in the Bad Boys Club. He was tired of getting pounded, especially by the meanest bully on the street, Butch Polnecek.

While the rest of the guys in the club played soccer in Ben Palmer's backyard, Nick sat on the outskirts of the playing area because he'd broken his stupid toe last week in gym class. Pushing his glasses up on his nose, he chewed on a piece of grass and studied the ad in the back of the comic book. Maybe this was the answer to his problems.

"Build bulk. Be a Real Man," Johnny Universe said in the ad. "I can teach you the secret magic formula to become a *real* man, and all it takes is twelve minutes a day."

It would be a dream come true to have muscles like Johnny Universe. Instead of running away, he could punch Butch in the nose.

Plus, he thought, as he read further, he would get three free gifts and a Real Man medal. Decided, Nick pulled a pen out of his back pocket and began to write his name and address in the tiny form.

A small shadow fell over him and he glanced up.

Olivia Polnecek. Considering she was Butch's little sister, she was a nice, but weird kid. Barely seven, she still played with dolls and liked cutting their hair.

Nick squinted through his glasses at the uneven fringe on her forehead and suspected she'd taken the scissors to her own bangs. Skinny as a rail, Olivia had big dark eyes, fine dark hair, and a red birthmark on her forehead. His mother called it a "stork bite." Her mother made her wear dresses all the time, and her knees were permanently skinned, probably from running from the worst brother in the world.

She looked so odd she was almost ugly. Even his mom said she was weird-looking. But Olivia was nice, and Nick felt sorry for her because Butch tormented her almost as much as he tormented him.

She rubbed her index finger and thumb together several times and shook her head, frowning. "I've been practicing, but I still can't snap my fingers."

"Use your middle finger with your thumb," Nick

told her, snapping his fingers. "And do it kinda hard."

She concentrated and tried again with no success, then flopped down beside him. "I'll never learn."

"Sure you will. You're still little."

"Not that little." She bent forward to look at his comic book cover. "Mighty Warrior Commandos. Is it any good?"

Olivia was cool about comic books. She liked all kinds, even bloody monster ones, and this was one more thing Nick liked about her. "Yeah, the Mighty Warrior Commandos are taken hostage by the Evil King of the Underworld. They can't use their secret powers to escape, so they have to trick him."

"Can I read it?"

"Sure—"

"Olivia." The terrible singsong voice of Butch permeated the sunny spring afternoon like a dark cloud. "I decided your Barbie dolls needed another haircut."

Olivia sucked in a breath of terror and jerked her head around to stare at her brother. Nick glanced at the bald, dismembered dolls and shook his head in disgust.

Olivia sprang to her feet and shrieked at the top of her lungs. *"My Barbies!"*

"I used them to reenact the battle at Pearl Harbor with my G.I. Joe dolls," Butch said. "The Barbie dolls were the casualties."

Olivia ran at Butch and yelled, "You're the meanest brother in the world. You're terrible. You're evil."

Butch held her at arm's length and laughed at her.

Indignant, Nick stood. He'd nearly always run from Butch, but he couldn't this time. Maybe that was part of becoming a *real* man. He jutted out his chin. "What kind of a jerk are you to pick on a little kid? Your own little sister?"

Butch scowled and turned his attention to Nick. "And what are you gonna do about it, you bad little boy?"

Nick started to sweat. "I'm gonna tell you to stop."

"You and what army?" Butch demanded, stepping directly in front of Nick.

Nick swallowed the lump of fear in his throat. "I don't need an army," he said, but thought he sure could use one. Butch was easily four inches taller and forty pounds heavier.

Butch pushed him hard, and Nick stumbled backward. It hurt his toe, but he didn't run. "Stop!"

"Make me," Butch said, and shoved him again, this time, harder.

Olivia ran between them and began to bounce up and down. "Leave him alone. You're just jealous," she said to Butch. "You're just jealous 'cause they won't let you play in their treehouse."

"Twit!" Butch said. "He's a wimp."

"He is not. He's smart. And if you don't stop, I'll— I'll—" She took a deep breath and stomped her foot. "I'll tell everyone *you have worms!*"

Butch roared in anger and shook Olivia by the shoulders.

Nick did what he had to do. He had no other

choice. He put his head down and plowed into Butch's side, knocking Olivia free.

From the corner of his mind, he heard the voices of his buddies.

"Hey, what's Butch doing to Nick!"

"Butch'll kill him."

"We gotta help."

Butch took a quick glance past Nick's shoulder, then pulled his fist back and hit Nick square in the nose. Pain shot through him, blinding him.

Nick fell to the ground, the pain continuing to vibrate throughout his head. It hurt so bad he was afraid he would cry. He heard the voices again.

"Butch has worms! Butch has worms!" Olivia yelled at the top of her lungs.

Stan bent over him and winced. "Nail 'em Nick, you're bleeding!"

Nail 'em Nick, he thought dazedly. His Bad Boy Club name.

Ben leaned down. "Oh, wow. Do you think it's broken?"

Joey squeezed his shoulder. "You okay?"

Nick tried to nod, but he felt like cannons were firing in his head. "Yeah," he said, but he was lying. As the other guys circled around him, Nick decided if he ever got the urge to be a Real Man again, he'd better learn Johnny Universe's secret magic formula.

One

She was up late again, and so was he.

Nick Nolan moved away from his bedroom window, denying his curiosity about his new neighbor. Her image lingered in his mind. Every night she paced the length of her room, wearing a skimpy nightgown and carrying a book in her hand. A lamp silhouetted the bounce of her long brown hair and the curves of her body. He saw worry in her walk, which made him more curious. A student studying for an exam? She looked a little more mature than most of the college students.

Nick had his own reason for insomnia. His law practice would consume every waking and nonwaking moment if he let it. It went against his policy, but he'd taken an appointment after hours, and the teenage girl's scarred face had haunted him the rest of the evening. His body was tired from his recent workout, but his mind was already working on how he would manage the case, leaving him in a state of stimulated exhaustion.

Through his years in the legal profession, Nick had learned the unfortunate truth that the American judicial system didn't always get the job done the way it should. Criminals didn't always pay the consequences.

Tonight was a perfect example. The teenage girl had been hit by a drunk driver whose father was a wealthy, respected doctor. The driver had gotten off with a word of warning from the judge, and the teenage girl would be scarred for life.

That was where Nick came in. In civil court, the rules were different, and Nick had developed an uncanny ability to make the bad guy pay. Although there were plenty of cases where lynching was preferable, Nick concluded that hitting a guy in the bank account was the adult equivalent of kicking a bully where it counted. It caused pain, the victim was compensated, and Nick figured he'd helped balance the scales of justice.

He nursed his beer and slowly paced his own hardwood floor. Years ago, he had moved into the fashionable Fan district of Richmond, Virginia, because he hadn't been ready for suburbia. The houses were old and situated close together, the businesses a mix of old diehards and trendy upstarts, and the residents ranged from retirees to university students. The eclectic mix suited Nick.

One of his neighbors was a city councilwoman.

The other, an artist who rented an upstairs apartment so he could keep eating. The woman pacer currently occupied the artist's upstairs bedroom.

He glanced through his window once again and saw her with a towel wrapped around her body. She must have just taken a shower. Her hair in a tousled knot, she shook her head and it tumbled loosely past her bare shoulders.

The towel fell to the floor, and for the first time in months, Nick forgot about his law practice.

Her neck was long and graceful, her breasts, lush and full. She was a little too thin, he thought, seeing the lamplight dance over her rib cage and narrow waist. Her hips and thighs had a welcoming curve.

She reminded him of what he'd done without for the sake of his practice. Hell, there was no shortage of women, he thought, irritated with himself. Since that damn article had appeared in the *Richmond Magazine* naming him Bachelor of the Year, he'd received so many calls he'd gotten an unlisted phone number.

The problem with the women swarming around him was that there was always something missing. He couldn't nail the exact quality that was lacking, and Nick had never been fond of taking just because he could, so he spent many nights alone.

His gaze transfixed on the woman, he felt a tug deep inside him. He wondered how her skin would feel against his, what he would see when he looked in her eyes. The deprivation burned and settled in his loins. He tried to blink, but couldn't make himself look away.

She held his attention as easily as she held the bottle of lotion or oil in her hand. Pouring it into her palm, she began to smooth it onto her skin. It was a cool night in November, and his window was cracked, but Nick felt warm.

With sensuous, yet careless strokes, she rubbed the oil down her neck to her chest and breasts. The tips of her breasts stiffened, causing a corresponding tightness in his gut. He would have lingered longer on her nipples with his hands, with his mouth.

She brushed the oil from her shoulders to her fingertips, between her fingers, and Nick found even the movement of her fingers intertwined arousing.

Her hands continued over her back and down her torso to her curved bottom. He sucked in a careful breath. She was the most sensual sight he'd ever seen. Her body was beautiful, but it was the way she touched it that affected him. Long enough to get the first breath of pleasure, but not indulgent.

He would want to indulge.

It occurred to him that she was trying to soothe herself, to massage away her apprehension. She probably had an anxious personality and wore her heart on her sleeve.

Messy, he told himself, his gaze still glued to her. She probably didn't hide her tears or laughter. Or her passion.

He took a careful breath at an erotic image that sizzled through his mind. He'd never needed to soothe a woman sexually. He'd never known a woman who had wanted that kind of tenderness from him.

Nick watched her lift one foot to rest on a chair. She worked the oil into her foot and calf, moving upward to the top of her thigh. The motion was both incredibly feminine and sexual at the same time.

Nick swore. He should look away. She was just a woman who studied her nights away. Just a woman with a body that turned his mind to mud. Just a woman with a bottle of oil. He wondered how her hands would feel on him.

Nick swore again. Where had that thought come from? Too much self-denial, he supposed, and looked away. He sipped his beer and thought about pouring it on his head.

This was ridiculous, he thought, and decided to pull his shade. Just as he started to tug it down, he saw her one last time in a sheer nightgown. She lifted her fingers to her lips as if she were taking medicine, then drank from her glass.

He frowned, but pulled down his shade and headed for his own shower.

The smell of smoke woke him. Nick sat up in bed and listened for his smoke alarm, but it wasn't buzzing. He climbed from beneath the covers and quickly checked every room of his house. No sign of trouble.

Returning to his bedroom, he thought of the woman who'd made him entirely too aware of his humanity, and lifted the shade. Smoke poured from an attic vent.

His gut tightened, and he reached for the phone. The 9-1-1 dispatcher took the call, but Nick knew lives were traded with seconds in these situations. Pulling on his jeans and a shirt, he pushed his feet into leather loafers, then ran down the stairs and across the lawn to his neighbor's.

He hammered on the door and yelled repeatedly, but no one answered. Nick wondered where Clarence, the artist owner, was. He wondered why the woman pacer wasn't answering. His last image of her drifted through his mind. She'd been taking a sleeping pill, he realized. Too sleepy to respond to the smoke.

Alarm trickled past his irritation. He pounded again, then decided to go in. The door lock was a joke, easily broken. Smoke filled the foyer. Yelling, he took the stairs two at a time to the second floor where flames kicked up in orange fury.

When a shower of sparks fell on him, he grabbed the metal banister where it curved at the top and immediately felt his palms branded. The heat and pain would have taken his breath if he hadn't been holding it.

She might be dead. The thought chased all others from his mind. Nick kicked in the door closest to his house. Her room was a fog of smoke. Bowing his head to inhale, he lurched toward her bed.

He took her in his arms and haphazardly threw the sheet over her. She was light and relaxed in his arms. Out cold. His chest tightened at the thought. That might not be good. Ducking down for one more draft of air, he sprinted out her door and down the steps. Loud sirens permeated the distinctive sound of licking flames.

He rushed out the front door and nearly stumbled over his councilwoman neighbor dressed in a bathrobe.

"Is it Clarence?"

Nick shook his head and snorted the cold, fresh air. "A woman. I think she must be renting from him."

"I thought he was supposed to be out of town. The wiring in his house is a mess. He should have replaced it years ago. He'll be lucky if he doesn't get sued."

"Yeah," Nick muttered, lowering the pacer to the ground. Adrenaline still pumped through his veins. Suing was his profession, but he was preoccupied with the woman in his arms. He wished she would stir.

"Is she okay?"

Nick didn't answer. He lifted the sheet from her face to see if she was breathing. She was, and still sleeping peacefully.

He shook his head. "That must've been some sleeping pill."

The sirens shrieked the arrival of the fire truck and the rescue squad. The crew was out of the vehicle almost before it stopped.

A med tech stooped beside Nick and immediately began to check the woman's vital signs. "She's unconscious?"

"I think she may have taken a sleeping pill."

He nodded and waved ammonia under her nose. She coughed and shuddered. Her eyes opened, alarm shooting through their dark centers. "What—what—"

Something about her eyes nudged at Nick. He studied her face. There was something familiar about her, a sweetness that almost made him feel nostalgic.

She looked from the med tech to him and back again, confusion tugging at her features. She lifted her hand to her forehead and pushed aside her hair.

With the light from the vehicles, Nick could see a mark on her forehead. A scar or a birthmark? He narrowed his eyes. A stork bite? A weird sensation rustled through him.

In a calm voice, the med tech told her what had happened and was asking her questions she was clearly struggling to answer.

"I—I was up late studying for my exam. I don't remember a thing after my head hit the pillow."

"Your name?" he asked.

"Olivia," she said.

The light instantly dawned, and Nick felt the oddest mix of emotions. "Olivia Polnecek," he murmured, staring at her in amazement. After all these years. He'd wondered what had become of her after his family had moved away from Cherry Lane.

Her forehead wrinkled in confusion. "Who are you?"

"He's the man who saved your life," the councilwoman told her. "He went into that burning house and pulled you out of it." She glanced away. "Oops. Is that a news team? I want to get dressed."

"News team," Olivia echoed with a cringe. She

sat up and pulled the sheet around her more securely. Still staring at Nick, she gave a slight shiver. "How do you know my name? Who are you?"

Inexplicably reluctant to tell her, Nick paused a half beat. "I'm Nick Nolan, your next-door neighbor."

Her eyes rounded in surprise. Her gaze quickly traveled over him and she shook her head. "Nail 'em Nick Nolan?" she said in disbelief. "But you don't look—" She broke off and searched his gaze. "You've changed."

"Yes," he agreed. He wasn't a scrawny, vulnerable kid anymore. As the adrenaline drained from his veins and his heart settled down, Nick began to feel a throbbing sensation in his palms.

"Hey, you've got a few burn marks on your face and arm," the med tech noted, reaching for his hand.

A shot of pain nearly buckled his knees. He grimaced.

"What's wrong?" Olivia asked, concern in her voice.

The med tech carefully lifted Nick's hands upward. Staring at his charred palms, he shook his head and whistled. "These will have to be dressed." He ignored the swarm of people running around, along with the reporter nosing closer. "Why didn't you tell me you burned your hands?"

Nick looked down at his hands as if they weren't his. The pain throbbed with every beat of his pulse. "I forgot."

* * *

Two hours later Olivia parked her overwrought body in a plastic orange chair near the front desk in the emergency waiting room. She wished she could park her mind. Her head was spinning. Since she couldn't get inside Clarence's house to get her clothes, she was wearing an old sweat suit a relief worker had given her. She had no idea where she would sleep tonight, let alone next week. Then there was the matter of her Western Civilization exam today.

Every other minute, she felt a slice of panic. She could have died in that fire. She might very well have died if Nick Nolan hadn't pulled her out. Thanking him was incredibly insufficient, as was offering him a ride home, but of all the things on her mind, Nick Nolan was on top.

He'd been hurt because of her. Her stomach twisted at the thought. She took a deep breath and couldn't help overhearing the conversation between the two admitting clerks.

"He's Richmond's studmuffin of the year, and when the press gets word of him rescuing his neighbor, the women will go after him like a cat after cream."

Olivia's attention was first caught by the words "rescuing his neighbor." Then the rest of the woman's words filtered through her mind. "'Studmuffin of the year'?" she echoed under her breath.

"The other lawyers don't call him studmuffin," the older admitting clerk said with a sniff. "Most of what they call him shouldn't be repeated. My brother is a bailiff and he told me that when lawyers find out they're going to be facing Nick Nolan, they don't go to court without putting on athletic cups."

Olivia felt a jolt of surprise.

"That man would be hard to handle, maybe impossible."

"Yeah, but it sure would be fun to try."

"Here comes the wounded warrior, now. Stop drooling."

Still digesting the conversation, Olivia watched Nick walk through the emergency waiting room with gauze-wrapped hands. She took a moment to look at him. There was almost a ruthless edge to him now, she thought, so very different from the boy she'd known on Cherry Lane. Tall, with broad shoulders and a lean, muscular frame, he projected power and strength. The strength appealed to her. The ruthlessness made her wary. The powerful image was amplified in the chiseled bone structure of his face. His stubborn jaw, intent gaze and posture emanated a masculine confidence that bordered on intimidation.

She could tell this man was no longer bullied into anything. She wondered if he could tell her the secret. Olivia had dealt with bullies, often unsuccessfully, during her entire life.

Refusing to bow to her own feelings of intimidation, she made herself stand a little straighter in the oversize sweat suit. "I thought you could use a ride home," she said.

His gaze met hers and he hesitated a second before he slowly nodded. "Thanks. I was just about to call a cab."

"It's the least I can do," Olivia said, leading the way to her car. "You did save my life." She glanced at the slight bump on his nose and winced. "My track record's not very good with you. This is the second time you were hurt while rescuing me."

He briefly touched his nose with his bandaged hand, then shot her a wry glance. "The first rescue was a turning point for me, and the fire wasn't your fault."

She opened the passenger car door for him and watched him fold his long legs into her economy automobile. She paused, looking into his eyes. "I'm very sorry about your hands."

He met her gaze for a moment, then glanced down at his bandaged hands and frowned. "Apology accepted. It'll be more of an inconvenience than anything. Who knows? Since I'm not one for random acts of kindness, maybe this will be the one thing that keeps me out of hell."

Humor, but no softness, Olivia thought, and concluded once again that the man was totally different from the kid she'd known. Although she was bursting with curiosity during the drive to his house, she kept her questions to herself when she watched him close his eyes. On impulse, she rode though a drive-thru window and bought a biscuit and coffee for him. When they arrived at his two-story home, he struggled with the key and she took it from him. She opened the door, and he swore colorfully. Olivia couldn't blame him. Bulky from the bandages, his hands were nearly useless. "How long do you have to wear the bandages?" she asked.

"A week or two," he nearly growled, then added, "Thanks for the ride and breakfast."

She could tell he would rather chew nails than ask for help. "I'll just take your newspaper and the bag into your kitchen." Passing through the spare formal foyer, she followed him to the kitchen. In a corner of her mind, she noted the neatness and lack of clutter. Neat freak, she thought with a trace of snooty disdain and grudging envy. It was her opinion that by nature of their personalities, neat freaks missed out on some of life's funniest serendipitous experiences. They also, however, always knew where their car keys were.

It wasn't her mission to help Nick Nolan have fun, she reminded herself. Tossing the paper onto his kitchen table, she glanced at the picture and caption on the front page. "'Prominent Attorney Saves Neighbor,'" she read out loud. "'Recently named Bachelor of the Year by *Richmond Magazine,* prominent attorney Nick Nolan rescued his neighbor from a burning—'"

Nick scowled. "Just what I need. I've already had to get an unlisted number because of that Bachelor of the Year bull, and—"

The phone rang. Olivia looked at Nick as he glared at the phone.

"Would you like me to answer it?" she asked after the fourth ring.

"No," he said. "If it's important, I'll get a page."

"Why don't you sit down and eat the biscuit, and

I'll scoot on out the door? Do you have any oversize plastic bags?'' she asked, pulling open the drawers.

"Top left drawer. Why?"

Olivia found them and pulled two out. ''Because they'll protect your bandages.'' She quickly unwrapped his biscuit, put the oversize plastic bags on his hands, and stepped back. Feeling his curious, brooding gaze, she wished she were wearing something other than a borrowed, baggy sweat suit. Something along the lines of Christian Dior. Or armor. She stepped back and mustered a smile. "There you go."

"What are you doing in Richmond, Olivia? College?"

Surprised, she nodded. "Yes, how did you know?"

He took a bite of his biscuit, then his gaze briefly swept over her again. "Lucky guess. Clarence usually rents to college students."

Olivia fought her recurring twinge of self-doubt about college. A twinge was far better than a mountain, and she'd worked hard to whittle her lack of confidence down to a twinge. "I got a scholarship. I love my classes, but it's been a long time since high school, and it's a little tougher than I'd planned."

"You'll get back into it. What have you been doing since high school?"

"Styling hair in Georgetown."

He chuckled, and Olivia blinked. It was the first expression resembling a smile she'd seen cross his face.

"Why am I not surprised?" Nick murmured. "Didn't you butcher your dolls' hair when you were a kid?"

"I didn't butcher," she corrected him as he finished the biscuit and gingerly lifted the coffee. "That was an early design phase. Pre-genius," she said tongue-in-cheek. "What about you? An attorney. You go after the bad guys?"

He took a quick sip of coffee and his smile faded. "I like to think so. Others would debate it."

"'Others' being the ones you've beaten in court."

"Yeah, I guess."

Complex, she thought, strangely drawn. Fascinating. His gaze gave the impression he could burn through the bull to the heart of a person, to the heart of a woman. Her heart gave an inexplicable trip. "Mighty Warrior Commando or Evil King of the Underworld?" she asked, referring to the days when they'd traded comics.

"Depends on the day," he told her. "I do what it takes to win."

Again she admired, even envied, his confidence. What kind of woman would he choose for his pleasure? she wondered. A cool, sophisticated, undemanding blonde, she imagined, and smiled to herself. If so, she was safe.

He cocked his head to one side, studying her. "That amuses you?"

Not quite, she thought, and felt her cheeks heat. "I was just thinking about Warrior Commandos. I should let you get some rest,'' she said. ''Is there something I can do for you?''

He shook his head and stood. ''Where are you staying?''

''I haven't really decided. The emergency services rep mentioned a couple of shelters.''

''A shelter,'' he repeated in a quiet voice that oozed disapproval.

Olivia registered his slight frown and a secret part of her marveled at his control. All the men in her life had only known one volume for revealing their negative emotions. Loud. Backing away, she shrugged. ''It's not a big deal. It'll just be for a few—''

''Stay here,'' he said.

He issued the invitation or *order* in such a reasonable tone, as if he wasn't a man who would be dangerous to *any* woman. Olivia stumbled, and Nick reached out to steady her, grimacing as his bandaged hands connected with her shoulders. She fell against his chest.

Upset that he'd hurt his hands trying to break her fall, she pulled back. ''You've got to stop doing this rescue thing with me,'' she told him. ''I've fallen lots of times before and gotten back up just fine. Staying at a shelter for a—''

''I didn't pull you out of that fire for you to stay at a shelter,'' he told her.

''I can't believe you're this protective on a regular basis,'' she said, wishing her heart rate would settle down.

''You're right. I'm not. Consider it a latent Warrior Commando urge. Stay here—'' He broke off when the phone rang. ''When you're not in class, maybe you can break the damn phone.''

After those final words, he strode out of the room. With the phone ringing like an annoying song that never ends, Olivia watched him climb the stairs and couldn't help thinking that Nail 'em Nick Nolan couldn't hide the truth from her. He'd grown into a Warrior Commando.

She was safe with him. Wasn't she?

TWO

"**Y**ou say you know there's a dozen women already calling him, but you want to be at the front of the line," Olivia said in a voice laced with amusement. "Actually, it's more than a dozen, but I'll be sure to give Mr. Nolan your message. 'Bye now."

From just outside the kitchen, Nick watched her hang up the phone. He hadn't rested long. His hands had kept him awake, and he resisted taking the pain medication that would send him on a long trip to la-la land. Nick guarded his privacy and solitude fiercely, so he wasn't sure what had possessed him to insist Olivia stay at his house. It must have been some insane protectiveness left over from childhood.

It had nothing to do with seeing her naked or rescuing her last night. Nothing, he told himself. When he took a second glance at Olivia's baggy sweat suit, however, he remembered the way her bare curves had gleamed with oil under her bedroom light. The sweat suit, he thought, should be buried.

"That's number seventeen," she murmured, clearly unaware of his presence. "I wonder if he's setting some kind of record."

Nick bit back a groan. "Not by choice."

Olivia jumped, and swiveled around to stare at him through the bangs that fell over her eyes. "I didn't know you were downstairs," she said, her gaze softly reproving. "I thought you were still sleeping."

"I don't need much sleep," he told her. Good thing, he thought, since he had more than his share of insomnia.

"Hands hurting?"

Dismissing the pain, he shrugged. "Who left the messages?"

She flipped through several sheets of paper. "Four local television stations and three radio stations want interviews. The rest were women with—" she cleared her throat "—assorted requests. Starting at the top. Kathleen, Melissa, Joan, Jennifer, Becky, Camille, Amy, Janece, Helen—"

"Helen," Nick said. "You can toss the others. What did Helen want?"

She glanced at him curiously. "Helen Barnett. Oh, she was the one with a sense of humor. She just said for you to call after you get some rest. Nothing urgent." She bit her lip as if she were fighting a grin. "Ms. Barnett suggested I tell the rest of today's callers to order a pizza from China. They would get a quicker response."

He gave a short laugh. "That sounds like Helen."

"Her number is—"

"I know her number."

"If you need me to dial it, I can," Olivia offered.

"She's on speed dial."

Olivia's eyebrows shot up. "Oh."

"Helen's probably one of the most important women in my life," Nick admitted, and waited half a beat for that to sink in. "She's my secretary."

Olivia blinked. "Oh."

Watching her changing facial expressions was so entertaining it almost distracted him from the pain of his hands. "You thought there might be some romantic involvement."

Olivia lifted her shoulder in discomfort. "Well, after all the calls I took from women who want to—" she pursed her lips together, looking as if she were searching for the right words "—terminate your bachelor status, I thought perhaps..." She muttered, then shrugged again. "I hate to think Kathleen, Joan, Jennifer, Amy and all the rest are pining in vain."

"They'll get over it," Nick said, walking toward the kitchen. "That kind always does."

" 'That kind'?" Olivia said, following him. "What if one of these women is your dream woman?"

Nick snorted in disbelief. "I don't have a dream woman," he said. "I don't have time."

Silence followed, and he glanced at her, expecting a lecture on the importance of love and romance.

Instead she nodded slowly. "I can understand that. Romance isn't a priority with me right now, either."

Surprised, he cocked his head to one side. "Your priority is school."

"Yes."

"But wouldn't you secretly like Prince Charming to come along so you don't have to go to school?" he asked, having repeatedly heard the common fantasy.

She smiled sweetly. "No. I would secretly like to graduate magna cum laude," she said in a husky voice that made his nerve endings ripple.

"What if your dream man comes along?" he continued, because she wasn't exactly what he expected.

"Good things come to those who wait," she said, then grew serious. "I want equal ground with any man when there are lifelong vows involved."

"This wouldn't have anything to do with beheaded Barbies, would it?"

She laughed. "Some," she conceded. "My father was hard on Butch. He had a tough time growing up. Difficult brother," she said.

"He was a difficult human being," Nick muttered. "Out of morbid curiosity, I wonder what he's doing now."

"He works in a nursery."

"With children?" Nick asked, appalled.

"Trees," Olivia said, a smile flirting with her lips again. "He's married and has three daughters."

"Outnumbered by four females," Nick said. "Justice at last."

"He's a little protective of his family, but I think his bullying days are mostly over." She studied him carefully. "When are you going to take your pain medication? You're hurting."

He shook his head. "Not that much."

She stepped closer and lifted her fingers a half breath from his face. For some reason, he held his breath. Her scent was both clean and sultry. He thought of the oil and felt his gut tighten.

"You keep doing mini-winces with your eyes. Let me get you some water," she said, turning toward the counter.

Uncomfortable with her help, he frowned. "No. I haven't decided to take it yet."

She turned around to look at him. "You're not one of those martyr types, or one of those men who thinks it's better to suffer?"

"It will knock me out for hours," he said.

"Isn't that the idea? I don't blame you for being grouchy," she said with a smile of understanding. "Your hands are bothering you."

A nurturer in a siren's body. If she were a little less emotional and a little more worldly, he might be in trouble.

"Some people think I'm always grouchy," he said.

She lifted her eyebrows. "They must not know you very well. Maybe you need a girlfriend, after all."

He felt impatient with her confidence that he wasn't a grouch. For all she knew, he could have grown into an ax murderer. He could tell she wanted to believe the best of him, and the knowledge both-ered him at the same time it soothed him. "Are you volunteering to be my girlfriend?'' he said to goad her.

He saw surprise, then a slight flicker of sensual assessment in her dark eyes before she quelled it. "I think you have more than your share of volunteers," she said in a smoky voice, then turned away and filled a glass with water. "Take your medicine. You want to sleep. You know you do," she said with a witchy smile.

When he looked at her mouth, he thought of all the ways she could use it to pleasure a man. Nick swallowed an oath. Was his mind playing tricks on him? Maybe he *did* need some sleep.

"I'll take the medicine," he said, "and call Helen before it has a chance to kick in. The doctor said if I take two of these, I shouldn't be feeling pain or anything else for a while."

As soon as he swallowed the pills, he pushed the speed dial for Helen and discussed the crisis du jour. This time, the opposition was trying to play musical chairs with the court dates. He studied his calendar and made a compromise.

"What a nice guy," Helen remarked with surprise.

"I'm just letting him pick the day he's going to die," Nick said with a slight grin.

He continued the conversation with some notes on a new client. Within minutes, though, he started to feel fuzzy.

At the beginning of his call, Olivia listened to the tone of his voice. It took her a few moments to identify what she heard. Passion. Nick had a passion for what he did. She had frequently heard that having a passion was one of the secrets to success. She wondered how Nick had discovered his passion. She wondered if she could learn something from him.

Watching him, she could tell the moment the medicine took affect. Nick rubbed his eyes with his wrists, then shook his head from side to side. Shifting around, he rested his head against the wall and began to nod in response to his secretary's conversation. Olivia waved her hand in front of his face.

He blinked, took a deep breath and rubbed the back of his bandaged hand over his face. "I gotta go, Helen. The light's about to go out. Page me if there's an emergency. I'll check in later." He dropped the phone into the receiver, then stood stiffly.

"Are you okay?" she asked.

He looked at her through his intense blue eyes and gave a slow blink that was oddly sexy to her. "Fine. I'm going upstairs."

Olivia watched him put one foot deliberately in front of the other, walking the same way a man who'd had too much to drink would. A trace of concern shot through her. "Are you sure you don't need any help?"

"No help," he said firmly, then took the steps with the same deliberate pace.

Arms folded, she stood at the bottom of the stairs, waiting for him to stop moving around. Silence finally. She exhaled in relief.

A loud punching sound vibrated from his room, followed by a string of curses. Alarmed, she bounded up the steps to his room, hesitating a half beat at his door before she burst into his room. "What is it?" she asked breathlessly. "What happened?"

Standing in the middle of his bedroom with his shirt torn apart and buttons on the floor, Nick swore again, glaring at his bandaged hands. "I can't even get out of these damn jeans."

Olivia's breath caught in her throat. His bangs fell over his forehead in sexy disarray, and his loosened shirt revealed broad shoulders, a well-muscled chest, and a flat abdomen.

He looked a little wild. The combination of his undiluted strength and frustrated determination did strange things to her insides. She shook her head at her reaction and took a deep mind-clearing breath.

"Let me help," she said, walking closer to him.

With heavy-lidded eyes, he watched her.

As if she were dealing with an undomesticated animal, she unbuttoned the cuffs and gingerly pulled his shirt sleeves down his arms and over his bulky bandages. She focused on his belt buckle to keep from staring at his bare torso.

He'd kicked off his shoes, but he'd gotten nowhere with his belt. Taking another careful breath, she bit her lip and unfastened the belt and the button.

It shouldn't have felt intimate, she insisted, but she felt too warm, inside and out. It was too quiet. Only the sound of his breath and hers broke the silence. Chatting would help, she told herself. She'd been a hair stylist for years. After her training, she should be able to chat her way through any situation, but her mouth felt dry, and she was struggling to keep her hands steady.

The hiss of the zipper as she slid it all the way down could have been a whisper of need. Too aware of her innocent brush against his masculinity, Olivia closed her eyes. His scent, natural and male, was sensual.

Moving her hands to the sides of his jeans, she carefully pushed them down over his hard thighs, kneeling to pull them off of his feet.

Done. She was all set to breathe a sigh of relief, when she felt his hand on her head.

"Olivia," he said in a gentle tone she hadn't heard from him in many years.

She glanced up the near-naked length of his body to his laser-bright eyes. "Yes."

"Thank you."

It's the least I can do. You saved my life. The thought echoed dimly in her head as she turned around and left his room. But she couldn't have formed the words if her next breath depended on it.

Olivia thanked her lucky stars her Western Civilization professor showed some surprising mercy and allowed her to take her exam later in the week. Between the fire and her morning with Nick, she had the concentration of a flea.

She gave herself a stern lecture on paying attention, then focused so hard during her next two classes she got a crick in her neck. No one except Olivia knew how hard she'd worked to get to this point. No one except her knew how terrified she was of failing.

Too many voices from her past had discouraged her.

"Boys don't like girls who are too smart," her mother had whispered to her.

"Learn a trade. You don't need college. You'll just end up getting married and pregnant," her father had said.

"Your standardized test scores indicate you might be better suited for vocational school than the college preparatory program," the high school guidance counselor had told her.

So Olivia had assumed everyone else knew what was best for her. She'd become a successful hair stylist with plenty of loyal customers, but she'd always secretly wondered how her life would have been if she'd gone to college instead. The wondering had grown to a burning desire. When she won the scholarship for her essay on the subject "Why College Is Important," Olivia knew her dream had grown wings.

"Now, if I can just get through my first semester of calculus," she muttered as she walked through Nick's front door with a bag of groceries and a backpack full of books. She immediately inhaled the strong pungent smell of smoke and wrinkled her nose. "What is—"

"Some of your clothes," Nick said as he leaned against the foyer wall, cocking his head toward two boxes. "Clarence brought them over."

"Clarence? I thought he was out of town." She raced to set down the bag of groceries on the kitchen table, then hurried back. "They smell awful. You should have made him leave them outside. I need to wash them."

"He said he'll replace anything that's ruined and he left you a hundred dollars. He'll bring everything else as soon as he can."

Amazed, Olivia blinked. "A hundred dollars? Clarence is nice, but he's—" She broke off, not wanting to insult her former landlord.

"Cheap," Nick conceded with a nod. "I talked to him," he said in such a casual voice that she almost didn't catch the darker undertone.

Olivia studied him again. He wore a black sweat suit with as much style as most men wore suits. Black suited him, she thought. There was a dark power about him. "You talked to him?" she ventured.

"Yes."

Stingy answer, she thought. "What did you say?"

"Not much," he said with a shrug. "Just pointed out the liabilities and possible costly consequences of faulty wiring."

She stared at him in disbelief. "You didn't tell Clarence I was going to sue him, did you?"

He paused. "I did not tell Clarence you were going to sue him."

She crossed her eyes. "We're getting knee-deep into legalese, aren't we? Okay. Did you suggest it might happen?"

"I discussed the possibilities and he became very motivated and concerned for your welfare."

"Wow," she said, shaking her head in amazement.

His careful-lawyer expression relented slightly. His eyes glinted with curiosity. "Wow what?"

Olivia laughed. "If you're this good after you've burned your hands and taken a double dose of pain medication, you must be pretty hot stuff in court."

"I do okay," he said, his lips flirting with a grin.

"And now you're going to be humble? Am I going to be able to afford this little conversation you had with Clarence?"

"We can negotiate a trade."

"Dinner?"

"Throw in the sweat suit you're wearing," he said, "and we've got a deal."

Olivia looked down at the dingy sweat suit in amazement. "You *like* this?"

"I'll use it to clean my car," he said, and left her staring after him.

The following afternoon, Olivia rushed in as Nick finished dictating a letter to Helen. Her dark hair swung around her shoulders as she walked past him in her clogs. Her body emanated so much nervous energy she almost buzzed. At the same time, she had a sexual aura that would make most men dizzy. She was not a calming woman. It amazed Nick that she could shake up his peaceful home without saying a word. "That should give him a kick in the pants," he said to Helen, feeling Olivia's gaze on him. "I'll talk to you later."

"Is this what you do every day?" Olivia asked, her gaze curious. "Compose threatening letters."

Nick felt a twinge of amusement. "I think of it as motivational correspondence."

She cocked her head to one side skeptically. "Motivational?"

"I'm reasonable. I give several opportunities to avoid meeting me in court."

"Do your cases usually go to court?"

"Not usually."

She looked at him for a long moment, and Nick suspected she was trying to decide how she felt about his career. Nick knew his ruthless approach made plenty of people uneasy, but it worked, so he felt no need to defend.

"You're a word warrior," she finally said, then her lips slid into a mysterious smile. "Do your clients ever fall in love with you?"

The way her mind worked intrigued him. "If it's a long, drawn out case, they sometimes get a little attached."

"And you? Do you get attached?"

He immediately wanted to say no, but it didn't quite ring true. "Early on I lost a case because I had a lot of sympathy for my client, but I didn't have a good plan. I can't get too emotionally involved," he said, "or it clouds my head. Injustice infuriates me, but strategy is how I win."

"But you have a passion for what you do," she said with a trace of envy. "You're luck—" The phone rang, and her eyes widened. She arched an eyebrow at him and smiled. "Would you like me to get that?"

He gave a deep nod. The amusement in her eyes made him want to stay and watch.

Olivia answered the phone and her smile broadened. "Stacy Evans," she repeated, giving Nick a questioning glance. When he shook his head, she grabbed a pencil. "You say you'd like to bring him a home-cooked meal. You're five foot eight, and won a contest for 'best legs' at a local bar. And you're blond. Okeydoke. Do you use double process to develop your color?"

He smothered a chuckle.

"Ah, highlighting," Olivia repeated, nodding her head. "Foil or cap?" After a brief discussion about touch-ups, she ended the conversation. "Of course. I can guarantee Mr. Nolan will receive your message. 'Bye, now."

She hung up the phone as she finished scribbling. "This one can cook, but it sounds like she might have a root problem."

Confused, he stared at her. "Why did you ask her all the questions when you know I'm not going to call her back?"

Olivia looked at her notes thoughtfully. "I've been rethinking your perspective on this and I think you could be wasting a great opportunity. Think about it. All these women are interested in you. When you *do* decide you want a date, if you keep a little information on the women, you can decide if you want to give one of them a call."

Nick was certain she had lost her mind. "They're all nuts."

"Maybe," Olivia conceded with a smile. "But they're nuts for you."

Nick shook his head. "They're nuts for who the media says I am."

She met his gaze and her smile softened. "And what's the difference between who the media says you are and who you really are?"

Nick felt the rough edge of frustration. When Olivia looked at him, he could tell she didn't see all the ways he had changed. She was still remembering that kid he'd been on Cherry Lane. Even as a child, she'd looked beneath the surface, a characteristic that irritated the hell out of him at the moment. "The media is making me out to be some kind of hero, a good guy, a *nice* guy," he said, knowing those days were long since passed. "I'm not a nice guy, Olivia," he said, and hoped she heeded his warning.

Nick lived in a bachelor's world. That meant the dry cleaner took care of most of his laundry and his meals were often take-out, from the freezer, or from a can. When the scent of a pastry baking in his oven wafted up to his study, he wondered if he was suffering from delusions.

He continued reading for the next few minutes, although the delicious smell grew more distracting than a noisy party would have been.

Finally giving up, he went downstairs and found Olivia bending to take a pie from the oven.

The voluptuous curve of her rear end made him forget about the pie. Nick knew that beneath the fashionably loose jeans, she had a waist any man would want to gently squeeze, a derriere that begged to be cupped in his hands, and silky thighs that conjured images of pleasure and satisfaction.

She had the kind of body that could drive a man

to distraction, but it was more than her curves. It was the way she moved, the way she smiled, the way her eyes flashed with her changing emotions that made him think of wild, unrestrained sex.

For just a moment Nick thought about taking advantage of the situation. Professionally, he was known for taking advantage of every situation. On a personal level, he'd quickly learned to choose women with a sophisticated mindset about sex who also knew how to keep their emotions in check.

The relationships sated his body, but left him with an underlying restlessness. He would almost say they left a void. Which was ridiculous, Nick told himself. He preferred to stay away from messy relationships and messy women.

There were always exceptions, he thought as he looked at Olivia again. She was emotional and unpredictable. He could tell just by the way she moved her body when she walked, she would be a sensual lover. Both demanding and giving, she would be a challenge. She wouldn't be easily controlled, and Nick was accustomed to being in control.

She would be a challenge.

Olivia whipped around to face him, her dark eyes wide with surprise, her face and blouse streaked with flour.

Messy, he thought. He might have changed since he was a kid, but Olivia still wore her feelings on her sleeve.

"You have a nasty habit of sneaking up on me," she told him.

Even her voice made him think of rumpled sheets

and bare skin. Her eyes, however, took him back to Cherry Lane. He reined in his dark urges. "The scent gave away your secret. I'm surprised the oven survived. No pies have been baked in there before. What kind?"

"Black cherry," she said. "But we should wait until after dinner. It's way too hot now."

An innocent comment, and Nick couldn't have agreed more, but he was thinking of a different kind of heat.

Three

"It's the least I can do," Olivia said, unable to watch Nick maul his slice of pie one more minute. She propped herself against the table and held the bite of pie in front of his mouth. "You did save my life."

Nick groaned. "Do we have to go through this again?"

She laughed. "No. You did great with the smoked turkey sandwich, but you're clobbering my pie. Quit complaining and eat it." He clearly hated needing help. "C'mon," she said. "You know you want it."

He shot her a dark glance that carried a sensual punch. She was so surprised at the heat in his eyes that she blinked, then his expression changed. He closed his mouth around the fork and took the bite. It was crazy, but even the decisive way he devoured the bite was sensually strong. Unfortunately, Olivia had learned that strength could be a cover-up for bullying. Nick, however, didn't strike her as a bully.

Watching his tongue skim over his lip made her stomach tighten. He made a low sound of approval, and she felt the sensation again. After he swallowed, she watched him for a long moment, distracted by her odd feelings.

He glanced up at her. "You're right. It's great pie. I want more than one bite."

A lick of awareness rippled through her. He would be a demanding lover, she thought. But would he be equally giving? she wondered. There was something incredibly seductive about the idea of being responsible for Nick's pleasure. She offered another bite and another, all the while feeling a tension inside her grow. He suckled a cherry with his tongue and she felt a flash of white-hot heat.

When the full knowledge hit her that she was unbearably turned on watching Nick eat the pie, she was appalled at herself. Where was her mind! Taking a few quiet, careful breaths, Olivia reminded herself that when she'd decided to go to college, she'd made some important decisions. During her first year, she had a no-men rule. She'd mentally flicked the switches to her heart and hormones to the off position.

When Nick finally finished the last bite, she was so unsettled she wanted to break the plate. Scooping it up, she wheeled around to the sink.

"That was great. Thank—"

"You're welcome," Olivia said quickly in a high voice and turned on the water.

She felt more than heard Nick behind her. Her heart hammered, and she bit her lip as she cleaned the dish.

"Any particular reason you're trying to scrub the paint off my china?" Nick asked in a casual voice just behind her ear.

Olivia felt every nerve ending in her back shimmy with awareness. She stiffened. "No," she said again in that quick, high voice that betrayed her nervousness. Olivia hated that voice. She rinsed the plate, put a determined smile on her face, and turned to face him.

His stance was easygoing, but Olivia was certain his laser-blue eyes took in every detail from her permanently tousled hair, to the color she knew was in her cheeks, down every curve in her body, to her restless feet. His gaze was so intent she wondered if he read minds. Dashing the thought, she turned up the wattage on her smile. "I'm glad you enjoyed the pie. I'm off to study for an exam."

He nodded, still studying her. "What subject?"

"Western Civilization," she said, eager to take the focus off her crazy thoughts and feelings even though she was anxious about her exam. "I know the material," she said as much for herself as for Nick. "But when I first look at the questions on the quiz, I go—"

"Blank," he said, nodding again.

Surprised Nick might understand her nerves, she

did a double take. "It's hard for me to imagine you going blank on anything."

"I didn't have a lot of exam anxiety, but I went blank a few times," he admitted. "Taking a few breaths, going on to the next question, and coming back later to the question that stumped me usually helped."

"I'll have to remember that," Olivia said, adding it to her little bag of tricks for surviving her first year of college. She was going to have difficulty remembering anything, however, if Nick didn't move away. Every time she breathed, she inhaled his scent and felt her hormone switch jiggle.

He leaned closer. "You don't look anxious," he mused. "You look more…" He hesitated. "Angry," he said.

"I'm not angry," Olivia said quickly.

His gaze flicked over her speculatively again. "Or turned on."

Suddenly mute, Olivia felt a slice of panic. *No, no, no.* She didn't want to be turned on, and if she was, she sure as heck didn't want him to know it. She should open her mouth to deny it, but the words stopped in her throat.

He cocked his head to one side and gave an almost-grin. "Bingo," he said in a low, velvety voice that held a tinge of surprise. "What tripped your trigger?"

He took a step closer, and Olivia found her voice. "Nothing. Nothing. Nothing. I'm not turned on."

His grin grew. "In my profession," Nick gently

told her, "I've learned that people often overemphasize when they're not being truthful."

Olivia took a deep breath and caught another whiff of his subtle sexy scent. She could dislike him for putting her on the spot. She jumped at that. Dislike was much safer than arousal. "It was temporary insanity," she said. "A quick flash of weirdness, and now it's gone. All gone," she added emphatically.

"Is that so?"

"Yes, it is," she said cheerfully, and prayed it was true.

His gaze grew curious. "What did it?"

"What did what?"

"Tripped your trigger?"

Olivia felt her cheeks heat and glanced away. "Oh, I'm not really sure I can put my finger on it."

"Was it something I said?"

"No, I just—"

"Something I did," he concluded.

Olivia groaned and closed her eyes. He wasn't going to stop. He was going to cross-examine her until she answered him. She opened her eyes and met his gaze. "Okay, okay," she said. "If I tell you, will you stop?"

"Stop what?"

"Badgering me!"

"Yes."

Spit it out, she told herself. "It was the way you ate the pie."

He gave a slow blink. "The way I ate the pie," he repeated as if she were speaking Portuguese. "But you fed me."

"Yes, but you really enjoyed it. There was some-thing…sensual about the way you ate. You devoured it—" she paused "—with a passion."

"The way I ate the pie," Nick said yet again. Olivia had been a weird little girl. She was now a kooky woman. Alluring, but weird. "And that's it."

He watched her sigh in exasperation and sorely wished for the use of his hands. He had a strong urge to pull her into his arms and taste her the way he'd tasted her cherry pie. He struggled with the urge, impatient with how much she appealed to him, im-patient with himself.

"Well, maybe the way you smell," she said grudgingly, then backed into the counter. "But it was temporary."

"A one-time anomaly," he said calmly, yet grow-ing more impatient.

"Yes." She nodded.

To hell with denial, he thought. It was just a kiss, a way to stop wondering about her. Nick had learned the reality of a woman was rarely as intriguing as the fantasy. He put his arms on either side of the counter, lightly trapping her. "If it's a one-time thing, we shouldn't waste it."

Her eyes widened. "Waste?" she squeaked.

He lowered his head.

"What are you doing?" she whispered.

"Curing some mutual temporary insanity," he muttered, then took her mouth with his. She stiff-ened, stunned, but after a second, she softened. He found her lips lush. She opened slightly, and he plunged his tongue into her mouth. Her taste was a heady combination of cherry pie and something more provocative. He wanted a little more of that taste.

Her soft little moan vibrated down his gut to his thighs. He rubbed his lips back and forth against hers, and she echoed his movement, gently pulling his bottom lip into her mouth.

He leaned his chest against hers and felt the hardened tips of her nipples through her shirt. What he wouldn't give to touch her breasts with his hands, but he was bandaged. Inhaling a quick breath through his nostrils, he continued to kiss her, eating at her mouth, letting her eat his.

On and on, he kept kissing her, wanting a little more. Just a little more, he thought, until she lifted her hands to the back of his head and began to wriggle slightly against him.

Nick grew hard. He rubbed between her thighs. She would be wet, he thought, and wanted again to touch her with his fingers. With his mouth. With his body.

Inch by mesmerizing inch, she trailed her fingers down to his hips and cradled his swollen masculinity against her.

"Oh, my word," she whispered, dragging her mouth from his, her eyes wide with distress. "I have to stop." She sounded as if she were speaking as much to herself as to him. "You have to stop."

Stop. His mind comprehended it, but his body was ready for action.

She squished her eyes closed for a second, then opened them. "I can't do this," she told him. "When I decided to go back to school, I turned my hormone switch to the off position, and it *must* stay that way! I can't fail!''

If it weren't for her extreme distress, Nick would have roared with laughter at the notion of turning Olivia's hormone switch off. Her anguish, however, tugged at his heart. That surprised the hell out of him because Nick had long kept his heart guarded better than Fort Knox.

"Whoa," he said. "What's this about failing? A kiss won't make you fail."

He watched her gaze flash with a dozen changing emotions, then she looked away. If he didn't know better, he would say she was close to tears.

"Olivia, what's this malarkey about you failing?"

He saw her brown eyes grow shiny with unshed tears she blinked furiously to hide. "Some people don't think it's malarkey," she finally retorted in a tight voice. "Some people think I will fail."

Nick felt a wave of protective fury. "*Some* people don't know much. In fact, many people don't know much."

"My family hasn't been very encouraging," she said.

"You're not surprised," he said, and heard the cynicism in his own voice. "Families can be a person's biggest support or biggest detractor. You're the one who is going to go to class and study. You're the one who is going to make this happen. No one else. One of the greatest pleasures in life is doing what someone else says can't be done."

He stopped abruptly, feeling a fleeting combination of self-consciousness mix with his conviction.

He sounded like a motivational infomercial, he thought wryly. But the light dawned on Olivia's face as if he'd struck a match and lit a candle. Damn if he didn't see hope and conviction stamped across her feminine features. "Okay," she said, then added in a voice that was sexy without her trying, "Mighty Warrior Commando."

As she walked to her room, he remembered her earlier comment about keeping her hormone switch on the off position and shook his head. She would need a cloak and a veil, and perhaps, a keeper.

Nick swore as he hung up the phone.

Olivia glanced at him warily. He'd walked around in a quiet, dark mood most of the afternoon. She didn't want to get too close to him, primarily because she was still appalled at how easily he had flipped her switch the other day. She was determined it wouldn't happen again. She would help him until his bandages were removed, then find another place to live. That was the least she could do.

"Problem?" she asked.

"Yes. Bob Dell, a partner from my law firm, has ordered me to make an appearance at a client's cocktail party. He says I'm 'hot' right now and wants to milk my popularity—fleeting though it may be," he added sardonically, "to get a big account."

"Maybe it won't be that bad. A few drinks and finger foods. With your bandages, you can probably even get out of shaking hands."

Nick stared at his bandaged hands and scowled.

Oops, she thought. Wrong choice. He reminded her of a tiger with a sore paw.

"If I'd wanted to play the political game, I would be working for the commonwealth attorney."

"No," Olivia murmured more to herself than to him. "You would *be* the commonwealth attorney."

He stared at her for a moment, then chuckled. "You're right." He sighed and shook his head as if he were resigning himself to an odious task. "I need to bring a date."

"Oh, well, that's no problem. We've got a mile-long list of women who are dying to—"

"Not in a million years," he said, waving his paw through the air. "I don't need that kind of complication. I need someone who understands this party is just a job," he said, giving her a brooding glance that made her uncomfortable.

The silence grew between them. Her stomach twisted at the way he was looking at her; assessing, considering. She picked up the list of female callers he'd received during the past week. "Are you sure one of these won't—"

"You," he finally said.

Olivia's heart bolted and she shook her head.

"You know I don't want any emotional involvement right now. I know you don't. It's Saturday night," he said as if the matter was decided.

"I don't think that's a good idea."

"Why?" he asked in a reasonable tone.

Because you're too sexy, too appealing, too strong. She bit her lip at all her unreasonable responses. "I just don't..." she said vaguely, then grasped at the first repeatable thought that entered her head. "I don't have anything to wear," she said, so relieved she smiled.

"No problem," he said without hesitation. "I'll give you my credit card and you can pick something up."

"Oh, no," she said, shaking her head. "I couldn't let you buy—"

"I insist," he said. "You wouldn't be going to the party if I weren't going. And I wouldn't be going if I hadn't rescued you."

Olivia gulped at his reminder. "Oh," she said weakly. "I guess it's the least I can do."

Nick's assistant, Helen Barnett, was a meticulously groomed, blond woman with more class in her French-manicured pinky fingernail than most women could ever hope to possess. Olivia put her age at forty-something and might have felt intimidated if she hadn't seen the warmth in the woman's eyes as they'd walked into a fashionable boutique on Libbie Avenue.

Olivia took a quick peek at some of the price tags and shook her head. "Oh, no. I'm definitely in the wrong place," she murmured.

Helen smiled. "Oh, but you're not. We should be able to find the perfect dress here."

Dismayed, Olivia looked at the rack doubtfully. "But they're all so…"

"So what?"

Olivia cleared her throat. "Expensive," she whispered.

Helen smiled again. "Nick said money is no object and sent along his credit card. You needn't worry about his credit limit."

Olivia's stomach began to churn. "I had planned to repay him."

Helen waved her hand dismissingly. "Consider it an act of charity," she said. "Nick makes a very healthy salary and doesn't take time to spend it. Not only that, you're the first normal woman to come into his life in a long time."

Olivia wasn't sure Nick would call her normal. "I still think there must be someone else more appropriate to attend the party with Nick."

"No. Nick hasn't come close to finding the right girl. I'm no matchmaker, but I've always thought the right woman for him will need to possess an unusual combination of qualities because he is definitely cut from a different cloth."

Curious about Helen's perspective, Olivia turned away from the clothes rack. "Cut from different cloth in what way?"

Helen cocked her head to one side thoughtfully. "He's almost too intelligent for his own good, and everyone knows he has the predatory instincts of a lion. In fact, one of the partners once talked about the different ways that lions and tigers kill. The lion crushes the back of his victim."

Olivia shuddered. "It's so hard for me to reconcile that image with the kid I knew when we lived on Cherry Lane."

Helen paused and her lips twitched. "You knew

Nick when he was a child? He didn't tell me. I must ask, what kind of child was he? A bully?''

Olivia shook her head, thinking of her brother. ''Not at all. Nick stood up to the bully. He even took up for me a few times.''

Helen gave Olivia another assessing glance. ''Then you know his secret.''

Olivia felt a dance of butterflies in her stomach. ''What do you mean?''

''Nick not only has the predatory instincts of a lion, he has the heart of a lion. But he keeps his heart out of reach and often neglects his leisure time. A shame, isn't it?''

Olivia thought about the past week she'd spent in Nick's house, and Helen's image of Nick clicked into place. ''Yes, it is,'' she said, but quickly reminded herself she couldn't—and shouldn't—do anything about it. The idea that Nick was missing out on the joy of life, however, bothered her.

''Oh, my goodness!'' Helen exclaimed, interrupting Olivia's internal debate. ''I have forty-five minutes to help you find something to wear before I need to get back to the office.'' Helen pulled out a black dress. ''Time to get moving. How do you like this?''

Although she agreed to try it on, Olivia searched in vain for the long, loose-fitting dresses she favored when she wasn't wearing jeans. In her previous life as a hair stylist, she'd worked in an exclusive but funky shop in Georgetown where the stylists had followed the owner's lead with casual dress.

Within thirty minutes, instead of a swirling campy

gown, Olivia was outfitted with a winter-white designer knit dress that skimmed her body in a way that made her grateful for the fact that the parking space she usually found forced her to hike to her classes. The coordinating shoes, bag and wrap completed the ensemble that cost about the same as two of Olivia's previous car payments.

"You still look uncertain," Helen said. "The color looks gorgeous with your complexion and dark hair."

"If I don't spill something on it," Olivia muttered, still ambivalent about the whole thing. She shouldn't be going to this dinner party.

Helen laughed. "You'll do fine. In that dress, you might even make Nick change his mind about not getting involved."

Olivia's heart jumped. "No! I don't want to change his mind. I don't want to get involved. I have a no-romance rule now that I'm going to college."

Helen did a double take. "'No-romance rule'?"

"Right," Olivia said. "I'm not going to get involved with anyone in a romantic way especially this first year I'm in college. I need to focus on my studies. I'm turning my hormones to the off position."

Helen smiled slowly, but looked doubtful. "Do you really think you can turn off your heart?"

Olivia felt her heart squeeze tight in her chest. "I have to."

Four

Tiptoeing on her new designer leather heels, Olivia saw him in the foyer. With his back to her, she couldn't help noticing the width of his shoulders beneath the black wool overcoat. His dark hair skimmed over the edge of the collar. Given his profession, his hair was just a little longer than it should be, she thought, and approved. Even from the back, she could see that he wore the fine clothes with ease.

With confidence, she thought again, and envied him yet again.

A split second passed and he turned. He stared at her so long she began to wonder if she'd smeared her lipstick or already run her stockings even though she knew she hadn't.

Unable to bear the silence a nanosecond longer,

Olivia cleared her throat. "Helen said you would be surprised."

"Helen was wrong."

Olivia felt a sinking sensation. "You don't like it," she said, caring what he thought and knowing she shouldn't. She cared far more than was comfortable. "I knew it was wrong for me," she said, mentally searching her wardrobe. "I—"

"No," he said, stepping forward and putting his gloved fingers over her mouth. "I didn't say I didn't like it. I'm just not surprised."

She shook her head in confusion. "I don't understand."

He gave a wry grin. "Olivia, you dress your body like it's a secret weapon. Maybe it is," he muttered.

Olivia felt her cheeks heat. "I dress comfortably."

"Baggy jeans, loose blouses, sweatshirts. You dress so you won't attract attention. That might work with other men."

"But not you," she said.

He shook his head. "I'm not surprised you look gorgeous." He lifted a dark eyebrow. "I'll have to beat off my colleagues. Now put on your wrap and cover yourself," he told her.

Olivia started to pull the cape over her shoulders, but Nick finished the task. "Thank you. I think. You look pretty wonderful yourself." She glanced at his gloves again. "How did you talk the doctor into getting out of your bandages?"

"Negotiation," he said with a shrug.

Olivia paused and looked at him again. "Does he *know* your bandages are off?"

"Yes. Surprised?"

"Yes, I didn't think he would agree to let you take them off yet."

Nick gave a low chuckle as he opened the door. "I didn't say he agreed."

Now, *that* didn't surprise her. Within moments they arrived at a posh west-end home where a man helped her out of the car, took Nick's keys and parked his car.

Olivia hung back when Nick started up the steps. He glanced at her and must have seen the uncertainty on her face. He returned to her side. "Look, if it helps any, I don't want to be here, either. We won't stay long."

"Okay," Olivia said. "But we never really settled exactly what you want me to do tonight." When he didn't reply, she sighed. "How you want me to act?" she asked. "As your date?" she elaborated, whispering the last word.

"Act?" he asked. "You just meet a few people, eat all the food you want and agree when I say it's time to go."

Olivia nodded slowly. He still hadn't answered her real question.

"You still don't look sure."

"Well," she said, fighting an attack of nerves. "I wasn't sure if I was supposed to act—" She broke off.

"Act how?" he asked, his patience clearly stretched.

"How affectionate I was supposed to act. I mean,

am I supposed to seem as if I'm in—'' She broke off again. "As if I *really like* you?"

He stared at her for a moment, then roared with laughter. "As if you *really* like me. Does that mean you *really* can't stand me?"

"I didn't say that," she said quickly, feeling her cheeks heat from embarrassment and indignation.

He lowered his head close to hers with a mock earnest gaze. "Tell me, Olivia, how do you *really* feel about me?"

To her dismay, her heart hammered so hard at his closeness she could barely think straight. She took a quick breath and caught a draft of his scent. "I feel like kicking you," she told him, then took the steps.

He quickly caught up to her and rang the doorbell. "What perfume do you wear?"

"I don't wear perfume. After I shower, I put on—"

"Oil." He said the word like a slow, velvet caress. "Yes. How did you know?"

He shrugged. "Lucky guess," he said, and the front door opened.

Soon after that, Olivia found herself separated from Nick. The hostess, Doris Tartington, along with the managing partner in Nick's law firm, Bob Turner, and a client, quickly surrounded him.

Olivia was introduced and forgotten, which was fine with her. She tasted a few appetizers, sipped champagne, and admired the lavish decor of the host's home. Several of Nick's colleagues introduced themselves to her. Three asked for her phone number. When she told them she was currently living with Nick, they disappeared before she could also reveal that she would be moving out soon.

After a while, she took Nick a glass of champagne and a small plate of appetizers.

He looked surprised. "Thank you," he murmured, and held her gaze for a moment.

"Nick, tell Mr. Crenshaw what you did with..."

Nick reluctantly swung his gaze toward his managing partner and held up his hand. "Just a second, Bob." He turned back to Olivia, cupped his hand at the nape of her neck and brushed his lips against her forehead. "It won't be long," he said.

Stunned by his touch and the brief caress, Olivia felt a rush of heat and just nodded. She wandered near the fireplace with a second glass of champagne and tried to gather her wits.

"Lovely party, isn't it?" an older woman said. "You're here with Richmond's reigning hero?"

Olivia hesitated, then nodded. "Yes to both. I'm Olivia," she said, extending her hand.

"Pleased to meet you. I'm Daphne Roget and you said you're Olivia?"

"Yes, Olivia Polnecek. Are you friends with the host?"

The woman nodded. "I've known them a long time. And have you known Mr. Nolan very long?"

Olivia chuckled. "About twenty years."

Daphne's eyes widened. "Since you were children. How sweet. And how is the grown-up Nick different from the child?"

Olivia thought of all the ways Nick was different

and of the way she hoped he wasn't different. "He's taller," she finally said with a smile.

"What kind of boy was he? Was he small for his age, or was he a big boy?"

"I always looked up to him," Olivia murmured, smiling as she remembered how kind Nick had been to her. "Even as a kid, he was smart and brave. He let me look at his comic books and tried to teach me how to snap my fingers."

"Did it surprise you that he grew up to be an ambulance chaser?" Daphne asked.

Olivia stiffened, and for a fleeting moment resented the woman's curiosity. Glancing at the crowd still surrounding Nick, she shrugged. At the moment everyone seemed to be curious about Nick. "I would never associate the term 'ambulance chaser' with Nick. He fights hard for his clients, and his clients are usually victims."

Daphne lifted her eyebrows. "You say that with such passion."

"Nick is passionate about his work."

"It sounds as if the two of you have a special relationship," Daphne said speculatively.

Olivia sighed. She hoped Nick would want to leave soon. She didn't like all these questions. "He saved my life in the fire," she told the woman. "I'd have to say there's never been anyone in my life like him, and," she added wryly, "there's never been anyone like me in his life."

"That was hell," Nick said as he drove home. "I shouldn't need to repeat it for a while."

"I would never have known you hated it," Olivia said. "From where I stood, you looked as if you were enjoying yourself."

Irritated by how the memory of her scent had affected him the entire evening, he shook his head. Visions of her naked and welcoming had taunted him despite his professional conversation. Every now and then he'd heard her laughter and wished he'd been talking with her instead of the prospective client. "From where you stood, you were too busy getting hit on."

"I was not," Olivia said. "When those guys asked for my phone number, as soon as I told them I was living with you, they may as well have vanished into thin air."

Nick pulled into his driveway. "I knew that dress would be trouble. You should have worn a sack."

"I would have chosen something looser, longer, and much less expensive, but your assistant insisted this was the perfect dress."

Hearing the offended note in her voice, he cut the engine and turned to her. "The dress isn't the problem. You are."

Olivia blinked. "Excuse me?"

"You're too sexy," he told her bluntly.

Olivia blinked again, then glared at him. "I am not."

"Yes, you are. The way your hair falls over one eye is sexy. Your eyes are commonly referred to as bedroom eyes. Your mouth makes a man think about a lot more than kissing. And to quote the host of the party, your 'body could stop every clock in Richmond.'"

"You're insane," she said.

"Then all the men at that party were equally insane," he told her.

She gave a put-upon, flustered sigh. "You're exaggerating."

"I wish," he said with a rough laugh. "If you want to get through your first year of college without attracting attention from men, think potato sacks."

Olivia rolled her eyes. "Maybe I will. Maybe I'll eat a cherry pie every day and shave my head."

"Good luck," he said. "If you took a course in ugly and studied every night, you'd still flunk."

"I don't want to be pretty," she told him. "I don't want to stop clocks or collect business cards from men I don't know. I want—"

"Business cards?"

She shrugged. "A couple of the men I met at the party gave me their cards."

He groaned. "If you don't want to be pretty, then what do you want?"

She looked achingly uncertain, heartbreakingly vulnerable. "I want to be smart."

His gut twisted. "You are smart."

"You don't understand because you have always been smart. Even as a kid, you were smart."

Nick looked at Olivia again and remembered her quiet, overly submissive mother, her autocratic father, and her bully brother. He wasn't into the psych du jour, but he supposed she hadn't had the most affirming background. In his eyes, however, she was like a gemstone in a bowl of rocks.

The air in the car was growing cool. He wanted to feel her close to him. It was crazy, but he wanted her to smile. "You know, intelligence is contagious."

She gave him a sideways skeptical glance. "Oh, really?"

He nodded. "Yes," he said, leaning closer. "It's like mononucleosis. Since I'm smart, if you kiss me, it will make you smarter."

Her lips twitched as if she were holding back, then she ducked her head and laughed. The sound rippled through him like bubbly spring water. "That's the worst, the absolute worst reason I've ever heard to kiss someone."

"You never know until you try," he said, sliding his hand behind her neck.

She met his gaze with dark eyes full of amused disbelief. "Could you prove this in a court of law?"

He gave a low chuckle. "You said I'm smart, so I should know."

Not giving her another opportunity to object, he took her mouth. Her lips were lush and sensual, and she tasted of champagne. The scent of her fragrant oil wove its dark spell around him. He tasted her again and again until she was tasting him back. The problem with kissing Olivia was that it made him want more.

He wanted her bare, against him. He wanted his still tender hands on her breasts, between her silky thighs making her wet and swollen. He wanted her restless hands on his bare skin, her seductive mouth on his body.

Olivia pulled back and took a deep breath, her eyes dark with arousal. "I feel a lot of things," she whispered, "but I don't feel smarter."

After a restless night, Nick woke early on Sunday morning and decided to review some briefs while he drank his morning coffee. He suspected Olivia was still sleeping. At 7:00 a.m., the phone rang. He looked at it warily, then quickly answered it.

"Congratulations!"

Oh, no, Nick thought. One of those fake contest winner dupes on a Sunday morning. "I'm not interested," he cut in quickly.

"Pardon? This is your neighbor, Anna Vincent."

The councilwoman. Nick winced. "Oh. Hello, Mrs. Vincent."

"I just read the paper about your engagement, and—"

"*My engagement,*" he yelled.

"Yes. In Daphne Roget's column. It's such a romantic story and—"

Although his blood pressure hit the roof, Nick's mind clicked into action. Daphne Roget wrote the local party column, and the woman was known to stretch and speculate. Nick thought her journalistic slant would be more appropriate for one of the *Enquirer* publications. Daphne had attended the party last night. In fact, he thought with a sinking sensation, hadn't he seen Daphne with Olivia?

"I haven't read the story," he said to Anna.

"Thank you for telling me about it. Have a good day," he intoned calmly.

He ran to the front porch for the paper and nearly plowed into Olivia, who stood at the foot of the steps, rubbing her eyes. "Is there a problem?" she asked in a sleep-husky morning voice that was entirely too sexy for a woman wearing a nightshirt with a pink bunny on the front.

"Possibly," he said, opening the door and grabbing the paper. He flipped past all the sections he usually read to Daphne's column and began to swear under his breath. "I want a retraction."

"What—" Olivia began.

The phone rang. Nick crumpled the paper and closed his eyes. "Suing isn't enough," he muttered. "I want her evicted from the planet."

"Hello?" Olivia said, and waited a second. "Wh-what?" she asked weakly.

Nick opened his eyes and watched her. She looked as sick as he felt.

"But we're not engaged," she said, then moved the receiver away from her ear as loud laughter rang out. She finally met Nick's gaze with wide eyes of distress. "It's the partner from your law firm." She held out the phone to Nick. "Bob."

Nick took the phone and didn't get an opportunity to breathe before Bob was calling him a sly dog and congratulating him. Several times, he tried to interrupt, but Bob was on a roll.

When Nick hung up, he squeezed the bridge of his nose. He wanted to punch something. "How long did you talk with Daphne Roget last night?"

"About twenty minutes," Olivia said, lacing her fingers together nervously. "She kept asking questions about you. I thought she must be a harmless, lonely woman."

"She is a society reporter with the instincts of a barracuda."

Olivia winced. "I'm sorry."

The phone rang again. Olivia started to pick it up, and Nick shook his head. "Let the answering machine get it. I need to know exactly what you told Daphne."

While the phone continued to ring incessantly, Nick listened to Olivia's recounting of her conversation with the society reporter. Olivia had innocently walked right into Daphne's web and supplied her with all the comments the reporter could use to twist and spin to create a completely fictional story.

"What is this bull about how I was always a smart, brave kid?" he asked, looking at the crumpled article.

Olivia shrugged. "She asked what kind of boy you were, and I told her I had always looked up to you."

As a kid, Nick had always been the runt. In the intervening years, all that had changed, but knowing Olivia had seen him differently even back then tugged at something inside him. He brushed it aside. "And what's this bull about you not having another man in your life like me?"

Olivia winced. "Well, you did save my life. And no one else has ever done that."

After that, Nick said very little, but his mind worked a mile a minute. Could he get a retraction or was the damage done? When Olivia finished the story, he checked his voice mail. With a sinking sensation in his gut, he listened to congratulatory messages from his assistant Helen, another partner in his firm, and a couple of his colleagues.

He abhorred the violation of his prized privacy. He considered his options and hated every one of them. Pacing from his kitchen to his foyer, he alternately swore under his breath and shook his head as the phone continued to ring.

Olivia bit her lip and stepped in front of him, the fragrant scent of her oil weaving its spell over him. Although she wore kneesocks and that oversize nightshirt, he couldn't help remembering how she had felt last night, how she had tasted. "This is my fault. Is there anything I can do? Do you want me to call Daphne Roget and—"

"No!" Nick said, feeling his blood pressure go through the roof. "No. Do *not* talk to Daphne again. If she approaches you, ask her about her liver ailment."

"I'm sorry."

"I am, too," he said, resigning himself to an imperfect course of action. "Everyone in Richmond thinks we're engaged. It looks like we have no choice."

"What do you mean?"

"You and I will have to become engaged."

Five

"*What?*" Olivia asked when she found her voice. Her heart was racing a mile a minute. She felt terrible for causing this mess, but surely she had misheard Nick. Surely.

"We have to get engaged," he said so calmly she could almost believe he was sane.

She shook her head from side to side in short, jerky movements. "No. No, no, no."

"It sucks, but it's the best solution," he told her. "Getting a retraction won't do any good now. My boss is practically turning cartwheels. It's not fun, but sometimes you have to do damage control."

Sucks. Damage Control. Olivia's brain replayed the words over and over. This didn't sound like a declaration of love. "It 'sucks'?" she finally echoed.

"Sure it does," he said. "I don't want to be engaged to you any more than you want to be engaged to me. That's probably the only saving grace in the situation."

He didn't want her. Her stomach twisted, but she told herself that was good because she didn't need his brand of madness. "Your flattery is overwhelming," she chided, "but I don't think this is a good solution."

"Given the options, it's best," he said, and it sounded so much like a decree she almost didn't question it.

She closed her eyes to his overwhelming confidence for a moment and reached inside herself. "I don't have time to be engaged. I need to stay focused on my classes."

"Then we're even. I don't have time to be engaged either."

Olivia groaned and opened her eyes. "Then *why* are we doing this?"

"Damage control. Sometimes you have to give the people what they want," he said, "before you take it away."

Olivia blinked. "What do you mean?"

He waved his hand. "It's temporary. We're engaged for a few weeks, then say it's not working and break it off. That will give you about a month to find a place you want to live."

A stampede of objections ran through her head. "But we would have to go to some social functions, wouldn't we?"

"A few," he conceded. "But everyone knows I'm a hermit, so it shouldn't be too many."

She would have to pretend to be in love with him in public. She would have to act as if she thought he was the most incredible man in the world. He would have to look at her as though he adored her. Her heart pounded against her rib cage at the same time her mind protested. Her sense of survival made a loud clanging noise. She licked her lips. "I don't think this is a good idea."

"Have you got a better one?" he asked in a direct, penetrating way that gave her some inkling of his court persona.

Olivia searched her mind futilely for *any* idea.

"I didn't want to pull this card," he told her, but there was a ruthless edge to his voice. "You owe me."

Her breath stopped in her throat. "For saving my life."

"No," he said with a frown. "For defending you and your Barbie dolls from your brother and getting a broken nose."

She slid the piece of paper next to his plate the following morning as Nick finished his breakfast of a bagel and coffee. Adjusting the backpack on her shoulder, she watched him from the corner of her eye.

He shoved his law brief aside and looked at the paper. "'Ground rules'?" he read out loud, then looked at her. "Is this a contract?"

Shaking her head, Olivia grabbed a bagel and popped it in the toaster. She hadn't slept well last night, and it had nothing to do with her classes and

everything to do with Nick. "Nothing that complicated. Just a few ground rules so you and I have our
expectations straight."

"'The engagement will last thirty days with an
amicable parting,'" Nick continued to read. "Sounds
like a contract to me. A primitive one, but..."

His attitude irritated her. "I didn't use legalese.
Do you still understand plain English?"

He studied her for a moment, then his lips twitched
ever so slightly. "I'll give it a try," he muttered.

"'The engagement shall not interfere with Olivia's
studies.' Okay," he said. "I'll buy that. What's
this?" he murmured. "'If Olivia's mother finds out
about the engagement, Nick has to explain the whole
story to her.' Why?"

Olivia felt every muscle in her neck tense. The
bagel popped up from the toaster and she gingerly
grabbed it and put it on a paper towel. "Because I
told her I wouldn't ever get engaged again unless I
was really going to get married."

"Engaged again? How many times have you been
engaged?"

"Just twice," Olivia reluctantly told him. "Both
disasters," she said, thinking that was putting a nice
spin on it. She took a bite of the bagel.

"Disasters," he murmured. "In what way?"

She swallowed the dry bite and reached for some
juice. "Do you really need to know?"

"I'm going to be your fiancé for the next thirty
days, so I need to know."

"Well, the first one lasted almost a year. I tried to
end it several times, but Brad was so nice and I felt

sorry for him. He was the youngest son of a wealthy businessman and his father had ignored him most of his life.''

''Brad?'' Nick prompted, sipping his coffee.

''Worthingham,'' she said, and watched Nick choke.

''These are the Worthinghams that own most of Maryland and Delaware?''

Olivia nodded. ''Yep. My parents have never forgiven me for not marrying him. They said he was major meal-ticket material. But it just wouldn't have been right. I didn't love him the way I needed to love him. He was nice, but he didn't have any goals. I needed to admire him,'' she said. ''And I didn't.''

''You could have been a wealthy woman if you'd married him,'' Nick said.

Olivia rolled her eyes. ''That's what my father says every time I go home. It would have been his money, not mine. I'm happier broke and sweating over calculus than I would have been with Brad.''

Silence followed. Feeling Nick's gaze on her, she finally looked at him and saw a tinge of fascination in his blue eyes. It was gone so quickly she wondered if she'd imagined it.

''You are an unusual woman,'' he said.

She shrugged. ''I never thought so.''

''The second engagement?''

Olivia sighed. This memory hurt. ''Bad judgment on my part,'' she confessed in a low voice. ''Very bad judgment. Sean was as driven as Brad wasn't. Unfortunately, he was driven in a way that involved illegal activities. As soon as I found out, I asked him to stop. When he didn't, I broke it off. Soon after that, he was caught and went to prison.''

Olivia couldn't meet Nick's gaze. She could look at his forgotten coffee cup suspended in his hand. She could look at his crisp white shirt and tie, his strong chin and jaw, even his broken nose, but not his eyes. To this day, she still felt ashamed of her poor judgment, and she hated the idea that Nick might look down on her.

''Everyone makes mistakes,'' he said in a quiet voice that surprised her with the warmth in its undertone.

''This was a biggie.''

''It could have been bigger,'' he noted pointedly. ''You could have married him.''

His words surprised and relieved her so much she felt a knot of emotion in her throat. She nodded.

''And you learned from it,'' he said.

She bit her lip, then laughed to push back the unwelcome urge to cry. ''Yes. I learned I have not-so-good judgment with men, so maybe getting engaged isn't a good idea for me. Look at the time,'' she said, changing the subject and wrapping the bagel in a napkin. She was going to drown if she didn't get out of here. ''I need to get to my class. So, are those ground rules okay with you?''

He glanced back at the paper. ''Only one left. 'Public displays of affection shall be kept to a minimum.''' He shrugged. ''The only danger is sex. It's not as if we'll get emotionally involved.''

Stunned that Nick could be so sensitive one moment and so utterly *male* the next, she gaped at him.

The last ten minutes she'd taken turn after turn on an emotional roller coaster. She took a careful breath and counted to ten. "That's where we disagree. Good sex and emotion go together," she said. "Otherwise it's just sex," she told him. "And it's not good."

She waited a moment, then decided to end the conversation. "I'm glad we understand each other. Have a nice day," she said, and headed for the door.

Nick caught up with her on the front porch. "I have a client coming tonight," he said to her.

She glanced back at him. "Does this mean you want me to fix dinner or drinks or something?"

He shook his head. "No. It'll be a teenage girl with her mother. The girl has some facial scars and doesn't want to be seen in public." He shrugged. "I don't usually meet with clients at home. I thought you should know they would be in the house."

She could tell from his expression that something about this case weighed heavily on him. "Okay. I can make myself scarce or hang around. Just let—"

"Nick and Olivia!" a woman's voice called.

Olivia turned her head to see Councilwoman Anna Vincent practically skipping across Nick's frost-covered lawn.

"Congratulations, you two," she said as she approached the porch. "I was delighted to read the news, Nick. I had begun to wonder if you would ever get serious with a girl. You must let me hold a party in your honor."

"No!" Olivia and Nick said in unison.

Olivia cleared her throat. "Thank you, but that's not necessary."

"Not at all," Nick added firmly. "Not necessary at all."

Anna shook her head and lifted her hands at their protests. "Of course it's necessary. When Richmond's most eligible bachelor gets engaged, it's cause for celebration. Or mourning for those other girls. Isn't that right, Olivia?" she added with a wink.

Olivia's stomach turned. "Right," she mumbled. "Well, I need to get to class. Have a good day," she said to Anna, then glanced at Nick.

An uncomfortable silence followed.

"See you tonight," he said, and slid his arm around her.

Olivia was so surprised she couldn't move, not even when he lowered his head.

"She's expecting this," he whispered, then kissed her.

At the touch of his mouth on hers, her heart raced. He pulled back slightly and she felt a shocking, unwelcome urge to cling to him. She felt a smidgeon of relief when she noticed Anna walking toward her house, but the controlled expression on his face bothered her. How could he remain so unaffected while she needed a fan? Angry at herself for her reaction and at him for his surprise caress, she bit her tongue to keep from sticking it out at him.

"I would appreciate a little more warning next time," she whispered, "so I can do a better acting job."

"Don't worry. You were very convincing."

Frustration boiled inside her, but Olivia didn't reply. She marched to her car, started the engine and made sure the windows were snugly closed. When she was two blocks away from Nick's house, she screamed at the top of her lungs.

By the time she returned to Nick's house early that evening, Olivia had decided that Nick had taught her something important. There were worse kinds of men than bullies. And Nick was one of them.

He was a dichotomy that made her crazy. Too intelligent, arrogant, clever, sexy, confident, heroic, occasionally sensitive, but often not, and just plain maddening.

The occasional sensitivity had gotten to her, she concluded. She'd let down her guard. Big mistake. Now she was having trouble with her hormone switch.

She tried to tell herself he was a jerk, but that was tough because the man *had* saved her life. She would just have to try harder, she vowed as she opened the front door and walked toward the kitchen. She would start tonight by spending the entire evening in her room studying calculus. Hearing voices in the living room, she recalled the visit with his client as she pulled a carton of juice from the refrigerator.

She poured a glass and turned around to lean against the counter as she drank it. She started when she spotted a girl with her head bent downward and straggly light hair in front of her face. "Oh, my goodness! You're so quiet, I didn't know you were here. Would you like some juice?"

The head gave a small shake. The girl hadn't made

a sound, but a smothering sense of loneliness seemed to surround her. Olivia would have to be totally insensitive not to feel the pain emanating from the girl.

Silence hung heavily in the room and Olivia remembered the rest of what Nick had told her. This was the teenager with the scars. For just a moment Olivia considered leaving the girl alone, but something wouldn't allow her to do it.

"I'm Olivia," she said. "I, uh, I'm Nick's fiancée," she said, and mentally added, *For a while.* "He's a terrific attorney. You're lucky he's representing you. Is that your mother in there with him?"

The head nodded again.

"You have an unusual hair color. Lovely strawberry-blond," Olivia chatted on, stepping closer. "I used to be a hair stylist, so I tend to notice hair. Has it been a while since you got it cut?"

Silence followed. "My dad's hair is this color," a muffled voice finally said. "It hasn't been cut..." She hesitated. "It hasn't been cut since the accident."

The flat tone of the girl's voice grabbed Olivia's stomach and twisted. "About three months?"

"Yes," the girl said, sounding surprised. She lifted her head a fraction. "How did you know?"

"I know hair," Olivia said. "But what I really need to know is calculus."

"You go to college?" the girl asked.

"Yes," Olivia said, and smiled even though the girl couldn't see it. "I'm twenty-six and I'm a freshman."

"You didn't go when you got out of high school?"

"No." Olivia hesitated. This particular fear was in the past. Admitting it wouldn't breathe new life into it. "I didn't think I was smart enough."

The girl lifted her head a fraction more, and Olivia saw the beginning of the red scars on her young face. The sight saddened her. At the same time, her mind raced with questions. How had this happened? What kind of accident had scarred her?

"This is supposed to be my junior year, but I don't know if I'll be able to catch up." She moved her right arm, which Olivia just noticed was in a cast. "I'm right-handed."

"How frustrating. I bet you've missed your friends."

The girl nodded. "I haven't seen them in a while."

"They haven't come around?"

"No. I—I haven't wanted anyone to see the scars. They're terrible."

Olivia knew she should be staring at calculus equations in hopes of someday understanding them. *And let this lonely, sad girl keep feeling lonely and sad.*

She couldn't have lived with herself if she'd left the room. Calculus could wait a few more minutes for her attention. It wasn't as if she understood it anyway. Sighing, Olivia sat next to her. "I don't have any scars," she said. "I have a birthmark right in the middle of my forehead. It's pinkish purple and about the size of a quarter. My mother told me it was called a stork bite and it usually goes away, but mine didn't.''

The girl glanced up to look at Olivia through overgrown bangs. ''I don't see it.''

Olivia smiled gently and rubbed off her foundation. ''The magic of makeup.''

The girl lifted her face. ''The doctors aren't sure what will happen with my scars. They just say it will take a while for them to heal.''

Olivia saw the red streaks across the girl's skin and took a sip of her juice to hide the emotions that rolled through her. Sympathy. Anger. Sympathy again. She tried to imagine how she might have felt if such an accident had happened to her when she was a teenager. She tried to imagine what anyone could have said to make it better, and absolutely nothing came to mind.

''What happened?'' she asked.

The girl's gaze slid away. ''Car accident. The guy who hit me was a drunk driver. He's fine.''

The injustice brought a bitter taste to her mouth. ''Fine,'' she echoed. ''Until Nick gets him. And he will.''

The girl met her gaze, and just beyond the bleakness of her pale eyes, Olivia thought she saw a flicker of anger. ''Yeah,'' she said.

''What's your name?'' Olivia asked.

''Lissa,'' she said. ''Lissa Roberts.''

''Well, Lissa, I've got some time on my hands,'' she said. ''How would you like a haircut?''

Thirty minutes later Nick found his client in Olivia's bedroom. The voice of Fiona Apple drifted from the radio. Olivia's shoes were tucked under a chair. One lone cookie and a few crumbs occupied the plate on the nightstand. Half-empty glasses of soda sat on the makeshift magazine coaster.

A tea party? he wondered, and took a second look. Lissa's hair looked different, and he noticed with surprise that she was actually talking. If he believed in sorcery, then he would say Olivia had worked some magic.

The two females sat on the floor surrounded by a beauty counter's supply of cosmetic pots and lipsticks and eye shadows.

Sitting with her legs crossed, Olivia used what looked like a paintbrush on Lissa Roberts's face. "It won't be perfect. It won't cover completely," she said while she painted Lissa's scars. "But if you get tired of the red, you can try this. It'll be better than trying to breathe through the scarf we tried earlier."

Lissa made a noise that sounded almost like weak laughter, causing Nick to stare. More magic? he wondered.

"Maybe I should move to Turkey," the girl said. "They wear scarves all the time there, don't they?"

Catching sight of Nick, Olivia gave him a lopsided smile. "Oh, hi. What do you think of Lissa's hair? She let me cut it."

"It looks pretty. I never noticed the color before," he said, thinking he'd never seen Lissa when her head wasn't tilted downward. Her hair had looked dull and misshapen.

"Here are my favorite Audrey Hepburn-style sunglasses," Olivia said to Lissa as she placed them on the teen's nose. "For when you feel brave enough to go out for ice cream. Or to a movie," she added, smiling gently, then turning to Nick. "All done with your appointment?"

"Yes, Mrs. Roberts is waiting in the study."

"Thank you, Olivia," Lissa said.

"Oh, this was truly my pleasure," Olivia said. "You saved me from facing calculus."

After Lissa's mother complimented Lissa's new cut and thanked Olivia profusely, they left. Nick glanced at Olivia standing beside him as she stared at the door.

"Will you win this case?" she asked, still not looking at him.

He saw the tension in her stiff body and heard the emotion in her voice. "There are no guarantees, but it's likely I can negotiate a sizable settlement for Lissa."

"That sounds like the kind of hedging you're instructed to use with clients," she said, crossing her arms over her chest and meeting his gaze. "I want to know what you really think."

The fire in her eyes echoed in his gut. She was angry about the victimization of Lissa. So was he. He just wouldn't let it control him. "You want to know if I'm going to fry the despicable excuse for a man who nearly killed Lissa. Yes, I am."

"Good," Olivia said, and paused for a moment, shaking her head as if she were reasoning something in her mind. "After that stunt you pulled this morning on the front porch, I tried to convince myself that you are an insensitive jerk without an ounce of tenderness, romance, or any other redeeming quality.''

Taken aback by her declaration, but still curious, he lifted his eyebrow. ''And now?''

''I still think you can be insensitive, and if you have an ounce of tenderness or romance, you hide it very well,'' she said.

''But I'm not a jerk and I have some redeeming qualities,'' he concluded, feeling a slight sting from her assessment.

She smiled, and he wondered why it made him certain the sun had peeked out from a cloud.

''You're a Mighty Warrior Commando,'' she said. ''You get the bad guy even after it looks like he got away.''

This wasn't blind hero worship. She spoke with confidence and conviction. The light of admiration in her eyes gave him the heady sense that he could conquer worlds. It was, he thought, more dangerous than any drug or sorcerer's spell.

Late that night Nick reviewed his notes as he sat in his room. Olivia had taken a shower in the guest bath and a teasing wisp of the scent of her oil lingered. He'd heard her pacing before she finally went to bed.

He'd worked out, showered, and paced to no avail. Although he would deny it to his dying breath, he was too spun up to sleep. Every time he looked at Lissa Roberts, he wanted to punch someone's face in. Every time he felt that urge, he reminded himself he would indeed punch someone, but in a far more crucial area. The bank account.

He shouldn't, however, have gone against his instinct to keep his home strictly off-limits to clients. It brought their worries and despair into his private domain. His home was his island of security, his personal haven.

If the Roberts case wasn't enough to bother him, the knowledge that Olivia was naked, soft, and shiny with oil, just a few steps away, put him over the edge. Her remarks about his insensitivity, and lack of tenderness and romance irritated him, challenged him.

Nick wasn't insensitive, and he could be as tender and romantic as the next guy. Well, romantic, anyway, he mentally amended. He just wasn't impulsive and stupid. If he were impulsive or stupid, he would be pounding down Olivia's door right now telling her to make love to him until his brain and body were numb.

Instead he would be rational while his body burned and his mind tormented him with the seductive possibility that Olivia could be his.

Six

"We have a social commitment Friday night," Nick said, nudging Olivia's shoes out of the walkway.

"So soon," she said with a slight grimace. She pulled muffins and roasted chicken out of the oven.

"Yes. You don't need to keep cooking for me," Nick told her. "My hands are better now. I can dial take-out again."

She shrugged. "It's a reciprocal response for me. I'm living in your house, so I feel like I need to do something."

Nick could suggest several other reciprocal offers she could make, but he refrained.

She glanced up at him. "Okay. What's the occasion? How dressy? And how adoring will I need to act?"

"Dinner with my boss and his wife. A dress will work." He ground his teeth. "Clarify 'adoring.'"

She scooted into her chair and he pushed it forward, enjoying the slight surprise on her face. "On a scale of one to ten," she said, "how much do I have to act like I think you are the smartest, sexiest, most incredible man in the world?"

Nick paused, his sense of fair play at war with his baser instincts. The idea of seeing how Olivia would act when she was crazy for a man was just too tempting. "My boss and his wife have been waiting for me to get married for years. They have repeatedly lectured me on the merits of matrimony. They want to believe this is the real thing."

Her face fell. "Ten?"

Nick nodded, and barely bit back a smile.

She wore a calf-length burgundy jacquard dress that nearly succeeded in hiding her curves, yet still gave the impression of easy sensuality. The only giveaway was the scoop neck that revealed the shadow of her cleavage. She wore her hair loosely tied back with a burgundy ribbon woven through it. She also wore an uncertain smile.

She looked sexy and vulnerable, and as Nick presented her to his boss, he felt the oddest sense of protectiveness. He kept the thought to himself since he was certain Olivia was liberated enough she'd kick him in the shin for his attitude.

"Bob and Karen Turner," Nick said, with his hand at the back of Olivia's waist, "this is my fiancée, Olivia Polnecek."

He felt Olivia stiffen for a second at the word 'fiancée,' but then she smiled and extended her hand. "I've heard so much about you. It's nice to get a chance to meet you."

Bob took her hand and patted it. "We're happy to meet you, but Nick's been so closemouthed we haven't heard a damn thing about you except from the newspaper."

"Bob, give them a break," Karen said with a gentle reprimand in her voice. "We can get to know Olivia during dinner."

The restaurant host called their party to guide them toward their table, and Karen turned to Olivia. "I understand you're a student at Virginia Commonwealth University."

And the grilling began.

"It's unusual to wait to start college when you did, isn't it?" Karen asked.

"Yes, it is," Nick intervened, taking Olivia's hand. "And it's one of the things I admire about Olivia."

Olivia looked at him and blinked. "It is? You do? Oh," she said, seeming to remember her role. She smiled and brushed his hand against her mouth. "Nick's support of my education is one of the reasons I fell in love with him."

Nick felt a tug low in his gut at the sight of her lips on his hand. Olivia turned the conversation to Karen and Bob's children. She charmed the couple by asking to see pictures and showing interest in Karen's volunteer activities and Bob's golf game.

All the while, she never missed an opportunity to

touch Nick—his shoulder, his arm, his hand. Several times, she smiled at Nick and held his gaze until Nick felt an insidious rush of heat and Bob cleared his throat.

He knew it was an act, but his libido and his body weren't nearly so rational. If he and Olivia were truly engaged, the evening would end with her in his bed. Her expressive hands would touch his bare skin. She would cup and stroke him intimately, and he would learn what made her gasp and moan. He would bury his face in her breasts and take her nipples into his mouth. He would slide his hands between her legs and make her warm and wet and as desperate for him as he would be for her. Then he would plunge inside her and brand her as his...

"I'd love to see your engagement ring," Karen said as they waited for dessert.

Nick tensed. *Damn.* He hadn't thought about a ring.

"We're looking," Olivia said quickly. "Nick said he wanted to give me something unique."

He played along. "Rubies," he said. "I thought something with rubies and diamonds would suit Olivia."

Karen sighed. "How romantic." She cocked her head to the sound of the band on the other side of the room. "Since the dessert isn't here yet, why don't we take a few turns around the dance floor?"

Bob made grumbling sounds of protest.

"Just a couple of songs. It won't kill you," she said, then turned to Nick and Olivia. "C'mon, you two. I know you won't mind."

Nick stood and shrugged at Olivia's tight smile.

"Of course," she murmured.

The band played an old Eric Clapton ballad, and Nick took Olivia into his arms. She was tense.

"Ease up," he coached against her ear. "You're supposed to be thrilled to be close to me."

"Oh," Olivia muttered, gingerly resting her chin on his shoulder. "Thanks for reminding me."

"You've been very convincing," Nick said, thinking she was no hardship to hold.

"Thank you. You haven't done too poorly yourself."

His lips twitched at her faint praise. "I think they like you."

"They're definitely curious about me. I almost felt like I was being interviewed. Should I have brought a resume?"

"No. That would have taken all the fun out of the interrogation."

He massaged the small of her back and lowered his lips to her throat.

She gave a soft, muffled gasp that ran through him like wildfire. "What are you doing?" she whispered.

"They're watching. We need to look like we're hot for each other."

She made a low sound of frustration. "How hot?"

Nick didn't hesitate. "Jalapeño hot."

She sighed. "Okay," she finally said, then lifted her head, looked directly into his eyes like a Valkyrie conqueror, and kissed the stuffing out of him. Consuming his mouth with her lips and tongue, she arched against him.

Nick felt his body temperature go through the roof while he grew hard and swollen. By the time she pulled away, it was all he could do not to slide his hands over her bottom and grind her against the part of him that throbbed with need.

Blinking a few times, she took a careful breath and managed a lopsided smile. "How'd I do?"

After they finally finished dessert, said good-night to Bob and Karen, and drove home, Olivia practically flew through Nick's front door.

"G'night," she called over her shoulder and ran straight up the stairs to her room. Closing the door, she stood in the middle of the floor and took several mind-clearing breaths.

With each inhalation, she breathed the subtle, seductive scent of Nick's aftershave. It wrapped around her and heated her blood the same way Nick had tonight when they'd danced. His scent clung to her dress.

Swearing, she stripped it off and tossed it onto the bed. "I'm never going to last," she muttered to herself as she paced in a circle, clad only in her bra, black stockings, and ankle boots. "It hasn't even been two weeks, and I *like* him!"

She grabbed a pillow and smashed it against her face. For her sanity's sake, she needed to hate him. It had been all too easy to pretend to admire Nick, to act as if she found him handsome and sexy. To kiss him as if she meant it. Kissing him had been stupid, very stupid.

Even now, she was still warm, still worked up.

Olivia's moan vibrated into the pillow.

Her vision obscured by the pillow, she kept moving because she couldn't keep still. Suddenly she snagged her toe under the corner of the rug and tripped. Forward, then backward. She landed flat on her rear end and shrieked.

"Olivia?" Nick's voice called from the door.

"Yes," she yelled, rubbing her bottom. She stretched out her legs to make sure she hadn't sprained anything.

"Are you okay?" he asked, cracking the door open.

Pulling the pillow against her chest, she stared at the opening door in horror. "I'm fine. I just tripped over the edge of the rug. You don't need to—"

He opened the door the rest of the way.

She scrambled to her feet and winced at the slight pain.

"Are you sure you're okay?" he asked in a doubtful tone.

Olivia looked at Nick and couldn't decide if he was a bigger pain in the rear than falling on the floor had been. He stood there in her doorway, so calm, so cool. So *dressed*.

"I'm fine. I fell where I'm best padded," she said, and hoped he would leave.

He didn't. His gaze trailed over her, as slow and as thorough as molasses.

"I'm fine as long as I don't need to sit. Thanks for checking on me," she said, hinting that he could leave now.

He stepped closer with a whisper of a grin that

spelled danger on his face. "I hate to think of you falling on your very nice rear end."

"I'll be fine," she said, resisting the urge to rub the part of her that still smarted.

"Need a second opinion?"

Olivia stopped breathing. The evening had been too much. His offer combined with the seductive look in his eyes put her over the edge. "Out!" she yelled, and whacked him with the pillow. He held up his hands and moved backward out of her room.

Not caring what kind of ridiculous picture she made with her stockings, ankle boots, bra and pillow, she glared at him. "Get out, you sorry excuse for a hero! Or Mighty Warrior Commando! Or *fiancé!*"

She slammed the door and threw the pillow against it for good measure.

From the other side of the door came a low chuckle. "All you had to say was no."

Olivia wanted to scream at the top of her lungs. Instead she counted to one hundred. Three times. Then after she was sure Nick was out of the hall, she did the only thing she could do.

She ran to the bathroom, stripped off her clothes, climbed into the shower and doused herself with freezing water.

The next morning Olivia got up and planned to spend the day at the library. She managed to beat Nick downstairs; no mean feat since he was an early riser. Glancing out the window, she looked mournfully at the sleet-covered streets. The ice sounded like needles hitting the windowpane. As desperate as she was to put some distance between her and Nick, she didn't want to put her car or herself in danger.

Alternative plan, she told herself. She would spend the day in her room. Making herself a pot of hot tea, she grabbed a muffin and rushed to get back to her room before Nick awakened.

As she reached the top step, he opened his bedroom door. Clearly just out of the shower, he stood in his doorway with damp hair, bare chest, wearing a pair of jeans and an assessing gaze on his clean-shaven face. Olivia found the sight of his muscular bare chest distracting, so she glanced down. His denim-clad hips and long legs proved equally distracting, so she looked up into his bright eyes and sighed. Everything about him was distracting, she thought glumly.

"You're up early this morning," he said.

Olivia nodded. "I was hoping to go to the Library to work on an English assignment, but the streets are a mess. I'll be in my room," she said, and started down the hall.

"How are you this morning?"

Olivia closed her eyes at her lack of manners. It was his naked chest, she told herself. He was more muscular than she had expected. She turned to face him. "I'm fine, and you?"

"Fine," he said. "And your—derriere?"

She willed herself not to blush. "Fine. I'm recovered."

"You won't need to sit on the pillow?" he continued, his lips twitching slightly.

"No."

"That was a very pretty bra you were wearing last night."

Olivia felt her cheeks heat at the image. "I would just as soon you forget last night."

"Not likely," he said in a dry tone. "But if you're going to work on an English assignment, feel free to use my computer in the study. The word processor on it is fairly standard."

Olivia stood silently for a moment digesting his offer.

He chuckled. "You look surprised."

"Well, I am." Chagrined, she quickly added, "And at the same time, I'm not. You have to be so tough and aggressive with your job that I forget how kind you can be."

For a moment she looked into Nick's gaze and saw the eyes of the kid she'd known and admired. A strange connecting kind of silence welled between them, and along with it a flood of nostalgic memories rippled through her mind. He had been so kind to her when they were children, and in a way, she had worshiped him. The thought disturbed her.

"Thank you," Olivia said, and slowly walked to her room.

It took a while for her to yank her concentration in line, but she spent the day in seclusion working on her assignments. Occasionally she heard Nick on the phone or walking in various rooms of the house, but she knew she had no hope of getting anything done if he was in the same room.

That evening before dinner, she took Nick up on his offer, booted up the computer in his study and typed the first six pages of her English essay. She saved the material, and was halfway through page seven when the power went out. With the room pitch-black, she waited for the electricity to return.

A moment passed and the beam from a lantern flashed across the room. "Tell me you backed up," Nick said, referring to the computer.

"I saved most of it. I learned about that the hard way," she said in a wry voice.

"Haven't we all?" he murmured, enjoying the sound of her voice in the dark. He moved closer and smelled the wicked, seductive scent of her oil. Nick was convinced her oil had been created to drive him insane. It was the oil, not the woman, he told himself repeatedly.

"No. I'm sure there are some people who have never lost one word because they always backed up with zip drive and floppy." She hesitated. "I would have thought you might be one of those," she said, and he could hear a smile in her voice. "Perfectionist type as opposed to a mere mortal type like me."

He shook his head and set the lantern on the desk. It lent a soft glow to the room. "Olivia, when did you turn into such a brash, mouthy female?"

She paused. "When I met you again. I'm only this way with you," she said. "Everyone else thinks I'm sweet, quiet, and shy."

He chuckled. "They don't know you like I do."

"They just don't *affect* me like you do."

He cocked his head to one side at her statement. "And how is that?"

Silence followed and she looked out the window

into more darkness. "Gosh, when do you think the power will come back on?"

"You didn't answer my question. How do I affect you?"

"I changed the subject."

"And I redirected. How do I affect you?"

Olivia groaned and bowed her head. "You make me want to scream."

"Really," he said, more curious than ever. "Why?"

"Nick, this is a crazy discussion to have anytime, let alone when it's pitch-black inside and outside."

"Indulge me," he said. "I've been looking at law briefs all day. I've been told I provoke my opponents to thoughts of murder, but I haven't heard anything about screaming."

"You're the most frustrating man I know," Olivia told him. "You're such a dichotomy. On one hand, you're this ruthless lawyer who refuses to be emotionally affected by his clients. You don't appear to have a romantic or sentimental bone in your body and make fun of those of us who do. On the other hand, you do things like rescue your neighbor from a fire and act as though it was the only choice you could make. You allow a badly scarred teenage client to come to your house because she can't face the world yet. And you offer the use of your computer to your fake fiancée."

She took a breath, then continued. "Plus, you're entirely too confident. Sickeningly confident," she said emphatically. "And you should be uglier."

Nick was speechless for five full seconds. He was

rarely speechless unless he was using silence as a communication tool. "I've never received so many backhanded compliments in my life. 'Sickeningly confident'?" he echoed.

"Some of it is job related," Olivia said. "But you have a deeper confidence a lot of people don't have. It's the kind of confidence that isn't defined by how you look, how much money you make, or what your occupation is. It's defined by who you are on the inside." She sighed. "You don't get that kind of confidence the easy way."

He heard the note of envy in her voice. "And you want that kind of confidence."

She gave a wistful smile. "Yes, I do."

Her vulnerability tugged at him and stroked an empty place inside him. Nick had eliminated any sense of vulnerability from his persona. It had been necessary for many reasons, and he'd never doubted his choice to close himself off until now. Olivia's openness drew him like a beacon in a dark night. Did she have something he'd been missing all these years?

He stepped closer to her and looked into her dark, dark eyes. "That's one of the most honest compliments I've ever received," he said, and shook his head as he lifted his hand to touch her jaw. "It amazes me how much you underrate yourself."

Her gaze held his for a long moment, searching and wanting. Then she looked down. "I once heard a story that confidence is for humans like flying is to birds. I think that means that some people are born with a great pair of wings, and they take off with no problems. Others have to get by on littler wings, or wings that have gotten broken along the way. They can still fly,'' she told him, meeting his gaze again. ''They just have to try a little harder.''

Nick felt something inside him shift and crack, one of many carefully erected walls built of stone. He felt a rush of profound emotion, the kind he guarded against. It was like salt water on a scraped knee. He could clearly see Olivia was the bird with a broken wing. For whatever reason, her family and the people around her had nearly convinced her that she couldn't live her dreams.

''You'll fly,'' he told her, struggling with a seductive yet wholly disturbing desire to give Olivia everything she'd never had. ''If anyone was ever destined to fly, it's you.''

Olivia stared at him, then horrified the hell out of him by bursting into tears.

Seven

Olivia threw her arms around Nick and sniffed. "That's the best thing anyone has ever said to me."

The heart-clutching intensity in her voice unsettled Nick. At the same time he felt ten feet tall. She felt warm and vibrant against him. Her tears dampened his shirt. Muffling a curse, he awkwardly patted her shoulder.

It occurred to him that many people believed in his potential. Many people had expressed belief in his ability to achieve his professional goals. Until now, he'd never realized how important that was. It bothered him that Olivia had gone without people who believed in her.

Olivia must have sensed his ambivalence. She pulled back and gave a small, watery smile. "I'm raining on your shirt. Sorry. I guess you hit a soft spot." She wiped her eyes with the backs of her hands. "The sprinkler's stopped. How about if I fix some sandwiches?"

"Thanks," Nick said, relieved the emotional pitch was taken down a few notches. "I'll get a fire started and we can eat in the den."

While Olivia went to the kitchen, Nick lit the fire and worked on quelling the strange restlessness inside him.

By the time he built a strong blaze, she appeared with a tray of sandwiches and beer. "I think these are turkey, but since it was pretty dark, I won't swear to it," she said.

"I'll risk it," Nick said.

She sat across from him and they ate in silence for a few moments. The firelight glowed on her face, emphasizing her exotic features. Neither classic, nor cool, she was striking in an unusual, unforgettable way. It wasn't just her face or her body, Nick thought. It was her spirit.

Spirit. He made a face at his thoughts. Where was that coming from? He glanced out the ice-covered window. There must be a full moon.

"There's something I've been wondering about you," Olivia ventured.

Nick swallowed a long drink of beer. "What's that?"

"When did you change?"

"Change how?" he asked, wondering where this kooky line of questioning might lead.

She put her sandwich down and looked at him.

"Well, you were always smart and brave," she told him. "When did you get so..."

"Insensitive? Callous? Ruthless?" he offered with a wry grin.

She covered her eyes with her hand in frustration, then peeked through her fingers at him. "I was thinking of the word 'tough.'"

Nick leaned back against a cushion and thought about her question. He recalled turning points in his career, in law school, college, high school, and even further back. "I think the day I started getting tougher was the day your brother broke my nose. I decided I was not going to be the little runt—"

"Runt!" Olivia said in disbelief. "You were *never* a runt. I remember you as smart and strong and brave."

Nick narrowed his eyes at her. Her face guileless, she wasn't joking. Olivia had never seen him as a runt, even when he had seen himself that way. An odd warmth suffused him. Not trusting the sensation, he shrugged. "I developed my competitive instinct when I wrestled in high school. Then I worked hard and played hard in college and law school. Once I started practicing law, I became even more focused because I wanted to win. Every time," he added with a grin.

"Helen told me one of the partners said you kill like a lion—breaking your opponent's back," Olivia said.

"Helen exaggerates," Nick said, and took another long swallow of beer.

"I don't think so," Olivia said. "She works with you and knows you too well to exaggerate."

"If there's anything the partners like about me it's my knack for speed. I know which buttons to push to get the opponent to move. Case in point is Lissa Roberts. The defendant's attorney didn't want to talk, until he received pictures of Lissa before her plastic surgery that will be an exhibit in court. Suddenly I'm popular. The defendant's attorney wants to talk with me."

Olivia smiled and leaned closer to him. "You're pretty darn good, aren't you?"

"I do okay," he said, more than ready to stop talking about himself. He sat up. "What about you? When did you change?"

Olivia grimaced. "I'm not always sure I did."

Nick laughed. "Sure you did. You don't look a thing like you did when we were kids. For one thing, your bangs are even now."

She groaned. "The truth is, I'm not that different. I hope I'm more mature, a little more careful about men, and more goal-oriented." She smiled. "But I still can't snap my fingers very well," she confessed.

"After all that time I spent trying to teach you? I don't believe you. Prove it."

She rubbed her fingers together and produced a very, very lame snap. "Told you so."

"By the time you were a teenager I bet you snapped your fingers and the boys came running."

"My father ran most of them off. He scared all my boyfriends. That will be one of the tests if I ever get engaged again. If I ever get *really* engaged," she emphasized, "the guy will need to be able to stand his ground with my dad."

"Good luck," Nick said. "If I recall correctly, your dad had a tendency to yell."

"And stomp," Olivia added. "His grown children secretly refer to him as the human earthquake. But speaking of snapping fingers, I think you're the one who snaps your fingers at women, then breaks all their hearts."

"Not me," Nick said. "I don't date women who have hearts."

"Why not?"

"Messy."

"And unsatisfying," Olivia said.

Nick nearly denied it, then shrugged. "Perhaps."

"You know what your problem is?" Olivia asked him.

"No, but I bet you're going to tell me," Nick said, and figured he'd have a helluva time trying to stop her.

"I think I know your secret. You act heartless and seem heartless. You can even look heartless." She lowered her voice to a whisper. "But you're not."

Nick felt her whisper tighten his gut like a silk string. His heart was safe, he told himself, even as it pounded hard against his rib cage.

"I could've sworn you said something about this deal between us requiring limited social engagements," Olivia said as the valet at the Jefferson Hotel in downtown Richmond took Nick's car keys and a tip.

"Comparatively speaking, this is limited," Nick said, ushering her into the grand hotel. "I receive an insane number of invitations. I'm not interested in attending these functions, but the partners of my law firm require me to attend some of them."

"Do you want to be a partner someday?" she asked, distracted by the ornate decor of the hotel.

"Yeah, for the money, the power, and the ability to torture some other new associate into attending these things," he said with a grin, then ran his gaze over her again. "I thought I told you to wear a potato sack to the rest of these parties."

Olivia rubbed her hands over her velvet-covered arms. She'd chosen the black velvet dress for warmth and versatility. "A potato sack to the Jefferson? But Elvis slept here," she told him.

He skimmed his fingers over her throat and the generous neckline that tended to fall off one shoulder without much urging. Olivia swallowed at his touch and his intent gaze. "Are you wearing a bra?" he asked.

She felt her cheeks heat and cleared her throat. "Uh, no. I can't because of the neck—"

"Do you know how many men," he asked as he ran his thumb over her collar bone, "you're going to drive crazy tonight?"

Olivia's heart raced. If she was going to drive a man crazy, she would want it to be— She slammed the door on that thought and bit her lip.

"Just don't collect any more business cards tonight. You'll stand out in that room."

Olivia frowned. "What do you mean?"

"If the women at this party were water, then they'd be bottled designer."

Olivia struggled with a pinch of inadequacy. "And I'd be tap water."

"No," Nick corrected her. "You're white lightning."

Leading her down a lushly carpeted hallway, he opened the door to a room where the party was in full swing. "Curtain call," he said, then wrapped his hand around her waist and kissed her.

It was a brief public claiming, but Olivia's brain shorted so fast she feared the people around her could smell her burning.

Nick's assistant, Helen, joined them and gave Olivia a hug. "Shame on you for keeping your engagement a secret," she said. "I almost bought that story you told me about keeping your hormone switch in the off position, but not now." Helen smiled. "You're going to be so good for Nick. Have you set a date?"

Olivia's throat tightened at the sincerity in Helen's voice. "A date?" she repeated weakly. "We haven't really—"

Nick slid his arm around her. "Olivia won't even discuss it until she finishes her first semester," he said smoothly. "And what do you mean, she's going to be good for me? I'm going to be good for her."

"Of course you will be," Helen said, "as soon as she makes you human." She waved a distinguished-looking gentleman to her side. "Paul Ginter, this is Olivia Polnecek, Nick's fiancée."

Paul took her hand and lifted it to his lips. "What

a pleasure," he said. "Exquisite. Perhaps you can use your influence on Helen to marry me."

Hearing Helen's soft gasp, Olivia blinked at the combination of the man's courtly manners and the twinkle in his eyes. "I'm not sure I have any influence," she said, uncertainly looking at Helen.

"Don't mind Paul. He gets this way every year. I think it's the mistletoe," Helen said.

Paul sighed. "She only wants me as her love slave."

Helen's color rose. "I think I'd like some champagne."

Paul immediately responded. "Your wish is my command," he said and, after giving a brief nod to Olivia and Nick, he escorted her away.

Olivia fanned herself. "Whew, he's pretty intense. What's their story?"

"Helen is a widow and Paul has been courting her for five years."

"Why doesn't she marry him?"

Nick laced his fingers through hers and tugged her toward a table laden with appetizers. "Her first marriage was long, but not particularly happy, so she's—"

"Chicken," Olivia concluded for him. "I understand being chicken, but that man—" She broke off and shook her head. "He'll be eighty years old and still making women sigh."

Nick grabbed a glass of champagne off a passing waiter's tray and offered it to Olivia. "You're going to have to explain this to me."

"Well, when he looks at you, it's like he really

sees you. Even that one moment, he took my hand, he gave me his undivided attention. Do you know how rare that is?"

"No," Nick said, wearing a skeptical look.

"I bet he's the kind of man who can make you feel as if you're the only woman in the room, maybe even the only woman in the world."

"How?"

Olivia shrugged. "I don't know. He looked into my eyes and took my hand and—"

Nick lowered his head closer to hers and lifted her hand between them. His bright gaze captured and held hers. "And?"

Her heart hammered against her rib cage and the rest of the room seemed to melt away. She felt a swirl of butterflies in her stomach. "And...and..." She swallowed as he lifted her fingers to his lips and kissed them. Holding her gaze, he ran his tongue over one finger.

Olivia's breath stopped somewhere between her lungs and her throat.

"And the randy goat said you were exquisite as he probably looked down your dress," Nick said.

Stunned, Olivia jerked her hand away. "You're impossible!"

Nick gave an infuriating chuckle and pulled her against him. "I'm not impossible. I'm just a jealous fiancé," he told her. "I want to be the man who makes you feel like you're the only woman in the room, in the world."

His words pulled at a soft spot inside her, releasing secret longings best denied. He was joking, she told herself. Recovering, she batted her eyes. "I guess you're gonna have to try harder."

A sexy, dangerous glint flashed in his eyes. "Okay," he said. "Just remember, you asked for it."

And the wicked games began. In between introductions, appetizers, and champagne, Nick didn't stop touching her. Subtle, sensual, affectionate caresses. He rubbed the inside of her wrist with his thumb when he introduced her to a colleague. He offered her a sip of champagne from his glass, then ran his tongue over the spot where her mouth had been.

He's not serious, she mentally chanted when her nerve endings stood on end and her skin felt warm and flushed. *He's not serious,* she repeated when she had to catch her breath at the way he made her feel. *He's not serious,* she told herself when her silly heart wanted to believe him.

She received a desperately needed break when Nick was reluctantly dragged away by a former client. "I won't be long," he promised next to her ear.

Olivia nodded. As soon as he left, she asked a waiter for a glass of ice water. Her mind was muddy, and if she had ever needed to be thinking straight, it was tonight. The waiter returned with her water and she took several swallows.

After a moment Olivia felt the itchy sensation of being watched. She glanced around her and encountered the gaze of an astonishingly attractive blond woman standing with several other people. Olivia smiled. The pretty blonde's mouth lifted in response.

"Some party," Olivia said.

"Indeed. I don't believe we've met. I'm Kendra Ross-Wilder. And you are?" she prompted.

"Olivia Polnecek."

"What a unique name," Kendra said, her tone neutral, then she introduced the four other people in her group. "I believe I saw you with Nick Nolan," she ventured.

Immediately reminded of her role, Olivia nodded and resisted the urge to cross her fingers. "Yes, I'm his fiancée." For a few more weeks. "Do you know him?"

"Oh, definitely," Kendra said with a too friendly smile, then shook her head. "I always thought it was such a waste that he chose civil law. He was incredibly bright and talented."

Olivia felt a twinge of irritation. "Nick is still incredibly bright and talented. He does an excellent job for his clients."

Kendra sighed. "But he could have gone far in politics."

Olivia didn't like the woman's deprecating tone. "Are you sure we're talking about the same Nick Nolan?" Olivia asked, and managed a laugh. "He would be bored out of his mind in politics."

The woman beside Kendra gave a soft gasp and Kendra's mouth tightened. "Of course I know Nick. We were quite close."

Olivia got the message immediately. Kendra and Nick had been lovers. She wondered if this was another one of the women with no heart. "Then you must know how passionate he is about his work."

Kendra gave a deliberate shrug. "It never made

sense to me. He's essentially become an ambulance chaser.''

Olivia felt one of her corks pop. Anger burned inside her. ''Nick Nolan is not an ambulance chaser. If you met the scarred teenage girl he's representing, or any of his other clients, then you wouldn't say such a thing. He's the last hope for people who have been screwed by the judicial system. He makes it right when things have gone very, very wrong.''

Despite the scrutiny from the growing crowd, Olivia refused to back down. Stiffening her spine, she stared straight into Kendra's eyes.

''Nick,'' Helen said to him as he tried to disengage himself from the charity organizer hostess of the party. ''You may want to check on Olivia.''

Hearing Olivia's name and the note of warning in Helen's voice, he cut off the conversation. ''Great party, Madeline. Nobody does it better. Thank you for including us tonight. I'll let you get back to your other guests,'' he said, and immediately scanned the room for a Gypsy dressed in black velvet.

''What's wrong?'' he asked Helen after they moved a few steps away.

''She met Kendra Ross-Wilder.''

Nick swore. Kendra was the stuffiest, snootiest witch on two feet that he'd ever had the misfortune to meet. Worse yet, he'd been so distracted by her breathtaking blond-haired, blue-eyed beauty he hadn't seen her diamond-hard heart. He got a sick sensation in his gut at the image of Olivia meeting Kendra. Kendra would rip her to shreds.

"How bad was it?" he asked, walking faster.

"After Olivia tore a strip off her for calling you an ambulance chaser?" Helen asked, nearly causing Nick to stumble.

He stopped. "Olivia did what!"

"From what I heard, Olivia put Kendra in her place," Helen said, an approving expression on her face. "Details get sketchy after that, but I heard the words 'cat fight' being whispered," she said with a slight wince. "Last I heard, Olivia was walking toward the coatroom."

"She didn't wear a coat," Nick muttered, and headed in the same direction. Down the hall and around the corner, he swiftly strode. He stepped through the doorway, stopped, and listened to the sound of footsteps in the back of the coatroom. He quietly closed the door behind him.

Moving to the back, he found her pacing up and down the last row of coats. Her cheeks colored from anger, her eyes shooting sparks, her fists stiffly at her sides, she reminded him of a female warrior. She had gone to battle for him, he thought, and felt a surge of possessiveness. He was accustomed to fighting his own battles, as well as other people's battles. He didn't need anyone taking up for him.

So why did it feel damn good?

"I understand you defended me to the Wicked Witch of Richmond," Nick said.

Olivia jerked her head up to meet his gaze with distress in her eyes. "I may very well have ruined your chances for pursuing political office."

Nick couldn't help roaring with laughter. "Politics?'' he echoed. "Me?" He chuckled again and walked toward her, wanting to kiss the wariness from her face. "If you've successfully managed to eliminate the requests I receive to run for office, the only thing I can say is thank you."

He searched her gaze. "So why are you hiding in the coatroom?"

Eight

Olivia's eyes shot off so much emotional wattage at the moment she should have worn a warning sign around her neck.

Clearly still volatile, she held up her hands when Nick moved closer. "I'm hiding in the coatroom because if I stayed out there any longer, I might need to hire you to defend me in court. I didn't think it would be a good idea to go outside. If I went to the powder room, I might run into—" her nostrils flared as she took a quick breath "—Kendra. I decided she wasn't likely to spend much time in here.

"She's beautiful," Olivia admitted as much to herself as to him, starting to pace again. "But smug. I've always had a hard time with smug people. The clincher was when she bad-mouthed you and your career. I wanted to dump a tray of meatballs on her."

She finally looked up at Nick. "I know she's beautiful, but how could you get involved with someone like that?"

Nick shook his head. He understood why Olivia would *not* understand. Olivia and Kendra didn't originate from the same planet, let alone the same species. "It didn't last long. She acted nice in the beginning. As soon as I found out she was determined to direct my career path, I bailed. She ended up marrying the son of a congressman. You can thank Kendra for shaping most of my attitudes toward romance. Now I try not to stand too close to her since I'm betting a house is going to fall on her one of these days. Just like the Wicked Witch of the West in *The Wizard of Oz*."

Her lips twitched slightly. "You call her the Wicked Witch of Richmond?"

He shrugged, relaxing at the return of her humor. "That's the nice description."

Her smile faded. "Were you in love with her?"

Nick sighed. His feelings for Kendra were distant and trivial to him now. "I was briefly in lust with her, but it's hard to stay in lust with a woman when you don't really like her." He paused for a moment while a strange realization sank in. "Unlike my feelings for you," he said.

Olivia's eyes widened. "What?"

"I'm in lust with you and I like you at the same time. Don't look surprised. You know I want to make love to you," he said when she appeared as if she might hyperventilate. "And you want me, too."

Olivia opened her mouth, but no sound came out.

She closed it and tried again. "I—I— That might be true, but—"

"I still can't believe you cut Kendra off at the knees for me."

Olivia winced. "Well, I'm not sure I cut her off at the knees, and she got a few shots in herself at the end, so…"

"What shots?" Nick demanded, feeling his sense of humor wane.

"She just asked me what I do for a living and made a couple of vaguely deprecating remarks," Olivia said, not quite meeting his gaze. "I think it was mostly for the benefit of the crowd around her. I made the last statement and left."

"What did she say?"

"I really don't want to talk about it."

Nick's stomach knotted. He could tell Kendra had in fact found a way to hurt Olivia. "Then what was your last statement?"

She still didn't look at him. "Do we need to keep talking about this?"

"If your remark was about me, isn't it fair that I know what it was?"

She gave a heavy sigh. "I said I might not know much, but at least I'm not stupid enough to call Nick Nolan an ambulance chaser when it's obvious that he is so much more."

Her words sank beneath his skin, to his bones, to the very heart of him. His chest tightened and he pulled her against him. "Oh, Olivia, she's not one-tenth the woman you are."

She finally met his gaze. "You don't have to say that to make me feel better."

"I'm not," Nick told her. "I'm saying it because it's true."

The vulnerability in her eyes kicked out the cornerstone of his restraint and he did what he'd been wanting to do too much lately. He took her mouth, and a little taste only made him want more. He rolled his tongue over hers. She molded herself to him as if she couldn't get close enough. She kissed him as if she wanted to consume and be consumed.

The restless edgy need for her that he'd buried inside himself threatened to explode. He slid his hands over her bottom, curling her into his hardness, and she instinctively meshed with him, moving sinuously.

In her mouth, he tasted her struggle, the barest hint of reservation and wild voluptuous desire. Filled with an overwhelming urge to possess her, he wanted to make the reservation disappear. He wanted to be inside her. He wanted her inside him. Maybe then, his gnawing need would be eased.

He slipped his hands underneath her dress to touch her thighs and rubbed his mouth over the softness of her throat.

"Nick—" she whispered in a breathless voice of both uncertainty and invitation.

He felt the rapid pounding of her pulse against his cheek as he slid the loose collar of her dress lower and lower until one full breast was bared. He stared at her, aroused by the sight of her erect, dusky-rose nipple.

As he lowered his head, he could feel her holding her breath, waiting for him. He took her nipple into his mouth and she moaned. Her fingers slid beneath his hair, urging him on.

The sensation of her in his mouth made him crazy. Pushing her stockings down her thighs, he sought her feminine secrets with his hand. Inside the silk of her panties, he found her wet and warm. It was all too easy to imagine plunging himself inside her. He stroked the swollen bead of her pleasure until she began to pant.

"Nick," she said. "This is crazy."

"It is. Do you want me to stop?" he asked, caressing the tender spot.

She gasped and closed her eyes. "No."

"I need more, Olivia," he said, and plunged his finger inside her.

She clenched and clung to him, shivering. "I—I need to be with you," she breathed, her eyes dark with desire.

"I want inside you as deep as I can get."

She wanted the same thing. He could see it on her face. Holding his gaze, she lowered her hands to his hard, aching masculinity. Sliding his zipper down, she cupped and stroked him.

It was an exquisitely sensual sight. Olivia with her gaze traveling to his bare erection. She rubbed her thumb back and forth in increments over the tip of him until a drop of arousal formed.

The sensation was so incredible he couldn't hold back a moan. Then, she lifted her thumb to her tongue to taste him. Nick nearly lost it.

Taking her mouth, he tasted himself on her while she slid her hand back around him and pumped. It was too much, he'd wanted her too long, denied himself too often. With her silken tongue sucking him gently into her mouth, she pushed him over the edge, and he spilled his pleasure into her hand.

Swearing, he wrapped his arms around her tightly. He waited for the aftereffects of sweet release. He waited to feel like he wanted her less. He waited, but he still wanted her. "I have to have you, Olivia. I have to make love to you tonight." He gazed into her eyes. She looked as needy as he still felt. "Say yes," he told her.

"Yes," she whispered.

During the drive home, Olivia kept wondering when her sanity would kick in. The cold December night should have cleared her head, but Nick had kept her warm by kissing her as he helped her into his car. Reason should have trickled in with the passing of time, but at the stoplights, he murmured sensual promises and stroked her swollen breasts through the velvet of her dress.

Where was her rational resolve? she wondered as she felt herself consumed by her need to be with him. There was a peculiar whisper of destiny to her making love with Nick, but Olivia pushed it aside for the louder voice of her desire and his. Her feelings for Nick were too complicated for her to comprehend, let alone name. Desire was easier to understand than destiny, easier to control than all the other things she felt. By the time they arrived at his house, however, she was ready to rip off her clothes and his.

They climbed the stairs in spurts broken by kisses and discarded clothing. "This isn't wise," she told him as they stood in front of each other naked in the darkness of his room. It wasn't wise, yet she was unable to keep her hands from his bare shoulders and back, unable to stop from rubbing her breasts against his hard chest.

"Not wise," he agreed, his gaze full of such intense desire that it took her breath. "But necessary." He picked her up and carried her to his bed.

The coverlet was cool to her back, but Nick's eyes and hands were warm. "Since you've been in my house, you've been an itch that won't go away."

Olivia felt a sliver of sensual apprehension. His wide shoulders blocked the light from the hallway and he was fully aroused. His power and strength moved her again. She sensed this would be no easy taking. "Itching?" She swallowed. "Are you sure that doesn't mean you're allergic to me?"

He gave a sexy, rough chuckle and followed her down onto the bed. "If I am, it'll mean you're responsible for another trip to the emergency room." He skimmed his hand possessively down her hip to her thigh. "Later," he added, and took her mouth and made her head spin.

He kissed her and caressed her with a passion that never abated. He left no part of her body untouched. His fingers made love to her skin, her nipples, her thighs. He made her wet and eager and scared at the same time. She wanted everything.

She couldn't hold back a moan as he slid between her thighs and took her with his mouth. Intimate kisses that sent her spiraling and crashing. He held her tightly when she cried out. He brought her a pleasure she'd never known. It was his combination of ruthless tenderness, however, that scored her heart.

He gently pressed his finger against her birthmark on her forehead, then leaned forward to press his mouth against the same spot. "I always liked this about you," he said.

Her heart still hammering, she searched his face. "Why?" she asked, thinking the way he'd touched her birthmark had felt as intimate as everything else he'd done to her tonight.

"You'll laugh," he said, lowering his mouth to hers.

Olivia felt his hardness against her inner thigh, the urgency in his kiss, and she was almost distracted. She turned her head to the side breathlessly. "Tell me."

He groaned against her neck, then with a resigned sigh, rolled back. He grabbed protection from the bedside table, put it on and finally met her gaze. "I thought a fairy kissed you before you were born and left a mark so everyone would know you were special."

She gaped at him in surprise. She would never have dreamed Nick would think such a thing, not even as a kid.

"Satisfied?" he demanded.

She nodded, still speechless, moved. Of all the explanations she'd been given for her birthmark, his was the most magical. Although she'd grown used to it, she'd always considered it a flaw.

"Good," he said, fresh arousal making his smile fade. "Then it's my turn." His gaze intent, he thrust inside her, and she gasped. "Too hard?" he asked, his jaw clenching with restraint.

She shook her head as she felt her body stretch to accommodate his sensual invasion. "No, you're just—" She wriggled and he grabbed her hips to still her.

"I'm just what?" he asked.

"Bigger than I expected," she said, closing her eyes and moving yet again.

Nick shuddered. "Oh, Olivia, I'm not going to last."

She opened her eyes. "You already have."

Nick shuddered again and began to slide in and out of her in a rhythm that threatened to take her mind.

The edges of the room blurred and there was only Nick above her and inside her. Only Nick. Again and again, he buried himself deeply inside her. With each stroke, she felt more taken. With each thrust, she felt her heart begin to slip.

Then he arched and his body rippled with release. As she held him while he shattered, she felt shattered, too. It struck her that even in that moment of vulnerability, he seemed so strong.

The silence in the room might as well have been as deafening as the thunder rolling inside her. Olivia began to tremble. She clung to him, wanting to hold on to the moment as long as possible. She didn't understand why everything still looked blurry until she felt a tear slide from her eye down her temple. Olivia had long accepted that she was an emotional person, but she wished for a thread of control at the moment.

Quickly batting her eyes to dry them, she took a long, slow breath. Nick's earlier words, however, twisted her heart. "Did you really think I was special when we were kids?" she whispered, almost hoping he would say no. His tenderness made her susceptible to him in ways she didn't know how to fight.

Nick lifted his face from the hollow of her shoulder and looked at her. "No. I knew it." He flicked his finger over her birthmark. "And I know it now."

Olivia squinted at the bright morning sunlight and quickly covered her eyes with her hand. She was aware of too many muscles and nerve endings in her body, a few she hadn't known existed.

He'd allowed her little sleep. Every time he'd made love to her, she'd been reminded of his strength, and with no darkness to hide her now, Olivia felt the edge of fear slip in. If she wasn't careful, she could lose her heart to him.

Turning her head, she slowly lowered her hand from her eyes and looked at Nick. She found no softness at the sight of him. His hair was slightly mussed from her fingers and his firm jaw roughened by a morning beard. His body was hard and muscular, too, as she intimately knew.

Even in sleep, he emanated power.

Olivia's stomach dipped, and she fought with uneasiness. He was too strong, too confident, too everything for her. His personality was so forceful she sensed he could swallow her up. She could get lost in him, and Olivia didn't want that. She'd known he was an innately strong and powerful man. Making love with him had reinforced the message a hundredfold. She must have been out of her mind to go to bed with him.

Suddenly his eyes slid slightly open and his hand reached out to snag hers. "Stop thinking," he said, pulling her hand to his mouth.

Olivia's heart bolted, and she stared at him. "How did you know—"

"I could hear you," Nick said in a wry voice, still moving his mouth over her hand. "You were thinking that last night has changed everything between us."

Last night *had* changed everything, but... She shook her head. "Actually, I was thinking maybe it's my turn for a trip to the emergency room."

He glanced at her in an assessing way that made her extremely aware of her nudity. "You look fine to me. Why the emergency room?"

She surreptitiously pulled the sheet up over her breasts and tried to retrieve her hand, but he held fast. "I was wondering if I might need a mental health professional."

"You're not saying you regret spending the night with me, are you?"

The possessive look in his light eyes made her heart race. "I, uh, I wasn't thinking of the word regret," she hedged.

When he kissed the inside of her wrist, alarm bells went off.

"Would you please give me back my hand?"

He nodded, then moved closer to her and touched her birthmark. "If you weren't thinking of regret, then what were you thinking?"

Olivia felt vulnerable and confused. She swallowed over a knot of emotion in her throat. "More like crazy," she whispered. "Very crazy."

He lowered his head, and she felt his lips on her forehead. Her heart squeezed tight.

"You can stay in my room," he told her.

Panic raced through her and she scrambled away from him, partly unwrapping the sheet that covered her. "That would be crazy, too!"

He narrowed his eyes. "So you think last night was a one-night stand," he said.

"Yes," she replied certainly, when she felt anything but. "Wasn't it?"

He held her gaze for a long moment, and she felt that strange sense of fate echoing inside her again. "It was a one-night stand," she said, trying to sound firm.

But Nick shook her soul when he shook his head.

Nine

Nick saw the alarm in Olivia's eyes and quickly rose from the bed to stand in front of her. She looked ready to bolt. He didn't want her to leave. If Nick believed in magic, he would say he and Olivia had made magic again and again last night. "You were incredible."

He watched her swallow. "No, I wasn't," she said, her voice wavering with nerves. "I wasn't incredible. I was just…you were just…" She took a deep breath. "We were just kinda worked up."

"'Kinda worked up,'" he repeated, and couldn't quite swallow his chuckle. "Olivia, that's like comparing a neutron bomb to a sparkler."

She jerked the sheet upward another inch. "Okay, we were very worked up, but that doesn't mean we should get worked up again."

"Do you really think one night is going to take care of what's between us?"

"Yes," she said.

Nick stepped closer. "I make a career of reading people sweetheart, and you're lying."

Olivia took two steps backward. "I don't think we should do this again."

"We can't go back after last night," he said.

Dragging the sheet, she hustled out of his room. "Yes, we can. I'll just go back to the guest room."

He followed her down the hall. "Olivia, this is crazy. We—"

"I agree! It's crazy and it needs to stop." She scooted into her room and used her door as a barricade. She peeked out of a three-inch space. "You were wonderful. Too wonderful," she said, her eyes welling with unshed tears.

His chest tightened at the raw emotion that vibrated from her.

"You don't want to be involved with me. I don't want to be involved with you. You don't love me, and I don't love you," she said with a slight wince. "I told you I had turned the switches to my heart and hormones off." She bit her trembling lip. "Stop messing with my switches."

He stopped messing with her switches.

Olivia told herself she was relieved. She needed to get back on track, to fortify her heart and focus on her studies. While Nick worked long hours on a case, she prepared for final exams. In quiet moments late at night, however, she struggled to banish the memory of how she had felt in his arms. She couldn't escape the feeling that she had belonged there.

After spending the better part of Wednesday cooped up in her room studying, she fixed a cup of tea in the kitchen. Nick burst through the front door, instantly dissolving the soothing effects of her first few sips.

"I won," he said, his broad grin contagious. He stepped around her shoes and continued toward the kitchen.

"Congratulations!" she said, feeling a rush of pleasure at his obvious exhilaration. She hesitated a couple of seconds, but stopping herself from hugging him seemed wrong. Wrapping her arms around him, she immediately felt the sizzle flare between them, so she pulled back and reached for the cup of tea she'd left on the table. "You're not surprised, are you?"

Nick held her gaze for a long moment, looking at her as if he knew all her secrets, as if he knew she fell asleep every night thinking of him. Olivia glanced down into her cup.

"I knew I would win. It just took longer than I wanted. Three years," he told her, loosening his tie and heading for the refrigerator. He grabbed a can of beer and popped it open.

"Three years," Olivia said. "I thought you were known for your speed."

"I am, and three years wasn't bad. Under normal conditions, it could have taken five years. This was a big case. The settlement involved a lot of zeroes."

"Five years," Olivia echoed, making a face.

"Gosh, that's longer than it will take me to get my degree. I don't see how you stand it."

He shrugged. "I do more than one case at a time and keep my eye on the finish line." He took a long swallow of beer and gave her a considering glance. "Sometimes after I cross the finish line, I celebrate with dinner. You game?"

The light challenge in his eyes made her chest tighten. She wanted to go. No, she didn't, she corrected herself. "I, uh, can't," she said. "I really can't," she added when his gaze turned skeptical. "I have a Western Civilization final tomorrow."

He paused and cocked his head to one side. "Rain check?"

She felt her chest tighten again. "If you like," she murmured.

"I would," he said. "In the meantime, where and when were the first European civilizations developed?"

Olivia blinked. How had he switched gears so quickly? She cleared her throat. "On Crete and other islands in the Aegean Sea around 3000 B.C."

"The idea of democracy spread—"

"During 400 and 300 B.C. in Greece," she said, feeling an odd rush of adrenaline at his pop quiz. "What are you—"

"But then a hotdog from Macedonia took over," Nick said.

"Alexander the Great," she said, shaking her head. "How in the world do you remember all this?"

"I had a minor in history," he said. "Want an A?" he asked. "Stick with me."

For the rest of the evening, she did. While they munched on sandwiches and snacks, Nick grilled her mercilessly on everything from the Roman Empire through the Middle Ages to the Renaissance. He made studying a crazy, playful duel that bolstered her confidence. By the end of the evening, he was throwing grapes at her for every correct answer she gave.

"Stop! I can't eat any more," she said, laughing.

"Full of the fruit of knowledge," he said.

"Full of grapes," she corrected.

A moment of silence stretched between them, and Olivia's emotions began to tumble through her. Before, the quiz had kept her feelings at bay. Now she realized she felt seduced by Nick all over again. She had begun the evening afraid of what she didn't know for the exam. Now she felt confident because of all she *did* know.

How had he done that? she wondered. How had he given her such a gift? And why? He could have had just about any woman joining him tonight as he celebrated his victory. Instead he'd stayed home with Olivia and helped her prepare for her exam.

Olivia took in the sight of his unbuttoned white dress shirt and ruffled hair. He hadn't even changed out of his work clothes. He *cared* for her. Butterflies danced in her stomach. "Thank you," she finally said.

He munched a grape, then swallowed. "For torturing you?"

She smiled and walked around the table toward him. "You do it very well. Torture," she stressed.

His lips twitched slightly, but there were layers of

darker emotions flickering in his eyes. "It's completely reciprocal."

He circled her wrist with his thumb and forefinger and, holding her gaze with his, he tugged her closer. It was so natural to lower her head and press her mouth to his that it was scary.

He sipped at her lips, sucking gently, exploring her with his tongue. She felt his kiss all the way to her toes. He wanted her. Her nipples grew stiff although he only touched her mouth and wrist. Her skin turned hot. When he slid his tongue in and out of her lips, she remembered another more intimate joining, and she felt warm and swollen between her thighs.

He must have sensed her arousal. She sensed his. Yet he pulled back and looked at her for a long moment. "Get some rest, Olivia. You're going to ace the exam."

Olivia took a slow, deliberate mind-clearing breath. "Thanks," she said, backing carefully away. "G'night."

As she climbed the stairs, she knew she owed him yet another thank-you. Two more seconds of his mouth on hers and all memory of western civilization would have been wiped out.

Nick opened the front door and immediately caught the spicy-sweet scent of Chinese food. Olivia bounded toward him, her dark hair flying behind her, her dark eyes shooting sparks of joy. "How'd it—"

She threw her arms around him. "I did it! I did it! I didn't just pass that exam. I conquered it!" She bounced up and down on the hardwood floor of his foyer. "I was *awesome!*"

Her exuberance spilled into him, making his chest fill with pride. He chuckled. "I bet you were awesome, Miss Olivia. Did you put out so much heat they had to call the fire department again?" he teased.

Olivia gave him a playful thump on the arm. "No, but I did great. And you're partly responsible."

"No." Nick shook his head. "You—"

"Yes, you are. Stop arguing. You do that all day," she told him, pulling him toward the kitchen. "I didn't have time to fix a real meal, so I picked up some Chinese and a bottle of domestic champagne. It's not much," she said, "but thanks."

Nick looked into her eyes and felt the kick of wanting all the way down to his stomach. Olivia was right. He should stop messing with her switches. She was too emotional, too unconventional, too vulnerable. The only problem was now that he'd had her, he didn't want her less. He wanted her more.

"It was my pleasure," he said, and joined her at the table.

They shared cashew shrimp, chicken lo mein, and rice. Nick couldn't tell if Olivia was giddy from her success or the two glasses of champagne she'd sipped. He only knew he couldn't take his eyes off of her.

After they read obscure messages from their fortune cookies, she insisted on refilling his glass and ended up spilling some of the liquid on his shirt. She gasped, looking instantly contrite. "I'm so sorry."

"It's okay," he said, unbuttoning the cuffs. "The shirt's cotton and was headed for the dry cleaner tomorrow anyway."

"That's good. I'm sorry," she repeated with twitching lips, "but if you hadn't moved your glass, I wouldn't have spilled it."

He did a double take at the gentle reproof in her voice. She was blaming him for her spill. Chuckling, he stood. "Is that so?" he asked, putting his hands around hers on the bottle and tilting it toward her chest.

Olivia gasped again, this time, when the cool liquid seeped through her shirt to her skin. She gaped at him in disbelief. "You dumped champagne on me!"

He chuckled. "I didn't dump it," he corrected her. "I spilled a little." Following a wicked impulse, he pulled the bottle from her and poured more on her. "That's dumping."

Her eyes widening again, she pushed at him. "I don't believe this. You're so neat and controlled and perfect, and you're making a mess!"

He put down the champagne bottle, silently agreeing with her assertion. He'd studiously avoided messes. Maybe that wasn't such a good thing. Still chuckling, he unbuttoned his shirt. "I'd forgotten how much fun getting into a mess could be. Here," he said, reaching for her. "Let me help."

"*Help!*" she howled. "After you dumped it on me."

He pulled her, squirming and slightly damp, into

his arms. "I just want to help you out of your wet blouse."

"And what else?" she asked in a dark voice, but she didn't move away.

His chest grew tight with the need to be with her, and his urge to chuckle faded. "Everything else," he said, lifting his hand to touch her cheek. "You know I want you."

A flash of need flared in her eyes before she squished them shut. She covered his hand with her own. "I thought you were going to stop messing with my switches," she whispered.

"I did," he said. "It didn't work."

She sighed, then opened her eyes and met his gaze. "What am I going to do with you?"

"I have suggestions," Nick said, lowering his mouth to hers. "But I'd like to start with you."

"Damn you," she said, then kissed him.

Her mouth was soft and sweet and hot. It all added up to a passion that fired in his belly like dynamite. Nick was accustomed to control, but Olivia not only made him lose it, she made him *like* losing it. He shoved the boxes to the side of the table, unfastened her blouse and bra, and gently pushed her back against the kitchen table.

He dragged his mouth down her chest and slid his tongue over her breasts, tasting the heady combination of her skin and champagne. He took her nipple into his mouth and gently suckled it. She rippled beneath him and tugged at his slacks while he pushed her jeans down.

Nick wanted everything at once. He wanted to take

her with his hands and mouth and body. He wanted inside her. *Slow down,* he told himself, sucking in a shallow breath of air. He grabbed the champagne bottle and poured a little on her belly.

She gasped, digging her fingers into his biceps. "What are—"

He watched the liquid slide down her abdomen and disappear into the mound between her legs. "Hold on," he told her, and followed the tiny drops all the way down with his tongue. He wanted every intimacy with her a man could share with a woman. He wanted to get as close as he possibly could get to her. He tasted her velvet soft femininity, stroking her and feeling her grow swollen beneath his tongue and lips. With each little sensual movement of her body, he grew harder and more needy. She slid her fingers through his hair and cried out in pleasure.

The taste and sound of her was so addictive he didn't want to stop. Over and over again, he took her with his mouth and pushed her over the top.

"Stop!" she finally begged in a husky voice. "I can't—" She shook her head helplessly. "I want—" Her dark eyes asked for everything her words couldn't. She skimmed her hand over him and Nick was again consumed with the primitive need to make her his.

He slid on protection, and thrust inside her. She squeezed his hardness with her silken femininity, and Nick followed her to a place where every sight and sensation centered around Olivia. Control spiraled away from him, and in the middle of his need to possess her, he wondered if she was possessing him.

* * *

The following morning Nick's alarm clock rudely awakened Olivia and him. He slapped the snooze button and reached for her as she moved for the side of the bed. "Oh, no, you don't," he muttered, pulling her against him. "I think I'll go in late today."

She chuckled, wiggling in his arms. "I bet you've never been late a day in your life."

Irritated that she was correct, he narrowed his eyes at her. "What makes you sure?"

"Because you are a superior man," she said, her gaze teasing and unwittingly tempting. "You wouldn't lower yourself to exhibit such a mediocre lapse."

"Superior, huh?" he said.

She pushed against his chest. "Yes, but you don't need me to tell you that. To tell you the truth, I've wondered how hard it must be for you to carry such a big head all the time. How do you do it?" she asked, batting her eyes innocently.

"Are you always cranky in the mornings? Or is it just because I'm going to leave soon and you won't be able to abuse my tender body and spirit until I get home again?"

Olivia thumped his arm, buried her head in his chest, and groaned.

He enjoyed the vibrating sensation of her mouth on his skin. "No reply? You're taking the Fifth already?"

"I'm not going to argue with a man who does it for a living."

He raised his eyebrows. "It hasn't stopped you

before. I think," he said, "I'm going to see how the other half lives and go in late today. Being human might not be so bad, after all."

She glanced up at him warily. "A first?"

"I never had a good reason before," he told her, anticipating the way her eyes widened slightly with nervousness. With what he had planned for her, Nick was pretty sure her nervousness was going to get worse before it got better. It was fair, he told himself, considering the fact that she had him twisted inside out. Toying with the strap of her flimsy pink sleeping gown, he smiled as he remembered pulling it from a drawerful of flannel nightshirts last night when she had insisted on wearing something to bed. "I got something for you," he said, and made sure his tone was casual.

"What?" she asked, all curiosity.

He shrugged and pulled them both into a sitting position. "Something I wanted you to have."

"That sounds vague," she said.

"Close your eyes," he commanded.

"I want to—"

"I thought you weren't going to argue with me." He gently covered her eyes with his hand and reached inside the bedside drawer for the small velvet box. Pushing back a sliver of concern that she might reject his gift, he pulled the ruby and diamond ring from the box. He felt her pry his fingers apart.

She gasped. "It's a ring!"

He grinned at the mixture of bewilderment and delight in her voice. "Yes, it is."

"It's beautiful," she said in awe. "Rubies and diamonds. Heavens, Nick, it's beautiful!'' She gingerly touched it, then immediately pulled her hand back as if she'd burned it. ''You can't...'' she began, shaking her head. ''I can't...we—''

''Can,'' he corrected, trying to quell her panic before it got out of control. ''I can and I did. It's just a ring, Olivia,'' he said, downplaying what it meant because he wanted her to keep it.

''Just a ring,'' she echoed, and blew her bangs off her forehead in disgust. ''You didn't get this out of a bubblegum machine.''

''It's not an engagement ring,'' he assured her. ''But when people ask to see your ring, you can show it to them.''

She looked at him with serious eyes. ''Nick, we're not going to be engaged much longer. My thirty days is almost over.''

Nick refused to acknowledge the way his gut twisted at her words. ''I know. That's why I said it's not an engagement ring.''

She shook her head in disbelief. ''Then what is it?''

He paused. She'd taken him off guard. A rare event for him. He'd known getting her to accept the ring would require some heavy-duty selling on his part, but he hadn't thought this far into the conversation. Any other woman would have had it on her finger already, he grumbled to himself. ''The ring is a gift, dammit. No strings attached. I want you to wear it all the time,'' he told her. ''Even after we're not engaged any more.''

''But—''

"But nothing," he said, his frustration growing. "This is a friendship ring. It makes perfect sense," he said. The rubies and diamonds, which reminded him of her fire and sparkle, seemed to mock him. "I sure as hell have never had a friend like you, Olivia, and I never will again. If I want to give you the freakin' Hope Diamond, it's my prerogative. There's no law against it. Now will you stop arguing and put the damn ring on your finger?"

Olivia blinked at him, then shook her head and smiled. She slid the ring on her finger. "You almost had me going for a minute, Nick. I could've gotten the crazy idea that this was some kind of romantic gesture. But you brought me back to reality when you started fussing." She shifted to meet his gaze and wrapped her arms around him. "Thank you, Nick," she said softly. "I want to be your friend forever."

Nick tightened the embrace. She wore the ring and was in his arms, but he wanted more.

Ten

Friendship ring.

After Nick left, Olivia couldn't sit still the rest of the morning. She didn't want to be alone with her doubts rolling around in her brain like a hundred Ping-Pong balls.

Rattled by the thoughts she didn't want to be thinking and feelings she absolutely shouldn't be feeling, Olivia resolved to keep herself busy the rest of the day. With her exams complete, all she could do now was wait for her grades. Lissa Roberts had been weighing heavily on her mind, so Olivia called the teen and invited her for shopping or a movie.

Lissa accepted, and Olivia followed directions to her house. As Olivia pulled into the Roberts's driveway, the sight of the ring on her finger distracted her. It was an exquisite piece of jewelry, and every time she thought about the fact that Nick had selected it for her, her stomach felt as if she were headed down the up elevator.

Friendship ring? Yes, they were friends. But they were also lovers. Olivia drummed her fingers on the steering column. Heaven help her, how had this gotten so complicated? What was going to happen to her heart when her thirty days was done?

A sharp sliver of fear cut at her and she closed her eyes to fortify herself. She was a survivor, she told herself. She had survived many things. She would survive this, too.

"Besides," she muttered as she got out of the car, "I'm *not* in love with Nick."

She slammed the car door loudly to silence the loud protest of her conscience. Lissa burst out the front door and ran toward the car like a bird that had been freed.

Lissa wore dark glasses and a hat, but the sight of the smile of the teen's face made Olivia's heart lighten. "Did you decide on a movie or shopping?" Olivia asked, waving at Lissa's mother.

"Both," Lissa said. "I went to a movie last week, and it was dark and great. No one even noticed me. I also want to buy some Christmas presents for my family."

The two of them got into the car. Olivia turned to look at Lissa. "Is it my imagination or do your scars look better?"

Lissa beamed. "I'm wearing makeup that covers the red, but the doctor said the scars may not be as deep as he'd thought. I'll always have some scars, but not as many and probably not as bad. It's just going to take forever for them to heal.''

''Forever?'' Olivia asked.

''Until I graduate from high school.''

Olivia made a face. ''I bet that does feel like forever. Have you let any of your friends visit you?''

Lissa nodded. ''Last week, my best friend before the accident came over. I was nervous and she asked a lot of questions, but she acted glad to see me. She's trying to talk me into going back to school.''

''Are you thinking about it?''

Lissa shook her head. ''No way. I can't stand it when people stare at me.''

Nodding slowly, Olivia started the car and headed toward the mall. Recovery was taking time, she thought, but there were signs of ''life'' in Lissa Land.

She took Lissa shopping first because the mall was less busy in the morning. They grabbed a quick bite to eat, then watched an early afternoon movie. Afterward, Olivia found a table in the corner of the food court while they ate ice cream.

Lissa looked longingly at a group of teenage girls laughing as they walked through the mall. ''I used to do that with my friends,'' Lissa said.

''You will again,'' Olivia said. ''You need time for your heart and your face to heal.''

''My mom wants me to see a therapist, but I don't want to talk about the accident. And I don't want anyone feeling sorry for me,'' Lissa said in a heated tone.

''You've been through a lot of trauma,'' Olivia said. ''Your mom wants you to get better.''

"I don't need a therapist."

"You might not," Olivia conceded, avoiding a head-on confrontation about an obviously sensitive subject. "Then again, you might just try it a couple of times." She smiled. "Kinda like going to a manicurist."

Lissa paused as if she were considering Olivia's perspective. She took another bite of her ice cream. "One thing I know for sure, I'll never get asked out by a guy again."

Olivia heard Lissa's need for hope in her fatalistic tone. "Of course you will. You'll date a few jerks, then you'll find a guy who loves your strawberry hair, your eyes, and your smile. And more importantly, he'll love you for surviving your scars."

"Is that the way Mr. Nolan is with you? Does he love you the way you always wanted to be loved?"

Olivia bit her lip. She felt like a fraud. Especially at this moment, she wanted to be authentic with Lissa. "He doesn't look at appearances only," she said, feeling honest, at least, in her statement. "That's part of the reason he's so special."

"You're lucky," Lissa said.

Olivia's smile felt strained. She didn't feel particularly lucky at the moment. She had to remind herself that she was indeed lucky to have Nick as a friend.

"Do you think you'll have babies as soon as you get married?"

Olivia's heart missed a beat. "Excuse me? Babies?" The image of her carrying Nick's baby made it difficult for her to breathe. "I won't have babies until I finish college."

"Does he mind?"

Olivia swallowed and winged it. "No. He wants me to finish my degree. He knows how important it is for me. My mother never did much outside the home because my father discouraged her, and Nick would never be that way with me. Never."

"It must be nice to have someone love you that much. You're lucky," Lissa said again.

Olivia smiled again, but it required a painful effort. She didn't know which bothered her more. That she felt dishonest by saying she and Nick were engaged, or that deep in her heart she knew the good things she'd said about Nick were true.

Arriving home from work, Nick opened his mouth to call out to Olivia, then stopped when he overheard her talking on the phone.

"Of course I'll be home for Christmas, Mom," Olivia said as she paced, shoeless, across the kitchen floor. "I just won't be home early. I agreed to, uh, house-sit," she said, crossing her fingers, "for the friend who is letting me stay here rent-free the rest of the month."

Silence followed.

"I expect my grades will be good," Olivia said. "No problem there. I'm glad I didn't try to work part-time this first semester, though, because some of the courses were tough." There was a brief pause. "No. Money's no problem," she said, crossing more fingers and rolling her eyes.

"Yes, I have another place to live starting January first," she said, crossing fingers on the other hand. She winced. "Yes, I'm staying away from the guys." She crossed two more fingers and closed her eyes. "Yes, Mom. I'm definitely moving closer to school in January," she said, uncrossing all her fingers. "I love you, too. Don't work too hard. I'll see you soon."

She hung up the phone and sighed. "Oh, what a tangled web we weave," she muttered. *"When we lie like dogs."*

Nick came up behind her and tugged a strand of her hair. "Do you need me to talk to your mom or dad?"

"No!" Olivia whipped around to face him, looking startled. "No. Not my dad or my mom," she said with a sick expression on her face. "I'm hoping they never find out about this."

He curved his hand beneath her hair and touched the soft skin of her nape. "Is it that tough to pretend you're engaged to me?"

"No," Olivia said again, too quickly. "Well, not as tough with people I don't know. But I want to be honest, especially with people like Lissa Roberts and my mom and—"

"Lissa Roberts?" Nick asked, wondering if Olivia was leading him on another conversational goose chase.

She nodded. "I took her out for shopping and a movie today and she started asking all kinds of questions about you and me."

"You persuaded her to go out?" he asked,

stunned. "Her mother said she refused to leave the house except for doctor visits. And they argued about those. What did you do? Put a spell on her?"

Olivia shrugged. "I think it was just timing. Lissa was getting bored."

"You're understating again," Nick said.

Olivia's brows furrowed in confusion. "Understating?"

"You do it a lot," he said. "You understate your effect on people."

"No, I don't."

"Yes, you do."

"No. I—"

Nick covered her mouth. "Do you really want to argue with a man who wins arguments for a living?"

Olivia glared at him, then nipped his finger.

Nick chuckled in surprise and pulled her into his arms. "Heaven help me, she bites!"

"I owed you," she said in a wry voice.

"Back to the original point," Nick said. "You do underestimate your effect on people." He shook his head. "Be careful about getting emotionally involved with my clients."

"You might as well tell me not to breathe. I can't imagine *not* being emotionally involved with someone who's been hurt like Lissa has." Sounding as passionate as he sometimes felt, she gave a smile that tugged at his heart and libido at the same time. "Good thing I'm not an attorney, isn't it?"

"Yeah," he muttered, sensing she was still unsettled about something. "What kind of questions did Lissa ask?"

Olivia groaned, pulling away. "She asked about you and your attraction to me. Then she mentioned—" She shook her head and looked slightly ill again. "Babies."

Nick's heart stopped. He took a careful breath and cleared his throat. "'Babies'?" he repeated in the most controlled tone he could muster.

"That's what I said," she told him, "after I nearly dumped my ice cream in my lap. I could deal with the ring, but the baby thing is going a bit far."

"What did you tell her?" he asked, curious as hell.

"Since you and I haven't discussed children," she said wryly, "I had to wing it. I told her you want me to finish my degree first because you know how important it is to me." She glanced away. "I told her if it was important to me, then it was important to you."

"That would be right," Nick said to her.

Olivia sighed and looked up to meet his gaze. "Sometimes it's hard being engaged to you when I'm not really engaged to you."

Nick nodded. "This is strange, but I know exactly what you mean. You and I would be a lot happier if we didn't have to deal with the rest of the people in the world."

"But the whole reason we got engaged was because of other people," Olivia reminded him.

"Yeah," Nick said, however his mind was filled with the image of Olivia big with his baby. He looked into her eyes and could see the brown-eyed gaze of his child. His heart tripped over itself and a warm feeling suffused him. He waited for cold panic, for rejection of the mere idea of children. He waited, but the warm feeling remained. A strange longing hummed through him.

Now, *that* made him nervous.

The following night, Nick and Olivia dressed for a Christmas party at Anna Vincent's home. As if both were aware their time was slipping away, they had stayed inside all day, hiding from the outside world and cherishing private moments. They talked and laughed, and with each passing hour, Olivia felt more vulnerable from the impact of Nick's undiluted attentiveness.

Nick met her at the bottom of the stairs. His gaze drifted over her appreciatively. "You look beautiful, but I can tell you don't want to go."

Although she felt frayed around the edges, Olivia mustered a smile. "You weren't supposed to notice."

He lifted a dark eyebrow. "That you look beautiful?"

She rolled her eyes. "No. That I don't want to go. You were supposed to be so overwhelmed by my beauty that you didn't notice anything else. But noo-ooo, you had to use your Warrior Commando super abilities and read my mind."

"Super abilities," he said with a dry chuckle. "It's more from years of taking depositions and learning how to read a face. We don't have to go tonight," he told her.

The intense passion in his eyes made her feel light-headed. She took a careful breath. "Yes, we do. Anna Vincent will disown you as a neighbor if we don't show. She's called three times today to make sure we're coming."

Nick cupped her chin. "We won't stay long."

The promise in his voice rippled through her. It would be so easy to grow accustomed to being with him, too easy to get used to feeling as if she belonged to him. She could learn to rely on Nick's undivided attention.

That would be a huge mistake, she thought, and looped her hand through his arm as they walked next door to Anna's festively decorated home. Anna's driveway and the curb in front of her home were filled with cars.

"Looks like Anna has a full house," Olivia said as Nick pushed the doorbell.

Nick nuzzled her neck. "That should make it easy to leave early."

Anna pulled the door open and smiled with delight. She quickly turned around. "It's Nick and Olivia," she called to her guests.

A hoard of people yelled, "Surprise!"

A few guests followed up with a singsong chorus of "Congratulations."

It took a full moment before Olivia comprehended the situation. Her stomach sank to her feet. "Omigod," she whispered. "A surprise engagement party."

"Kiss your bride-to-be, Nick. You're standing under the mistletoe," Anna said. "Then we can start the toasts and gifts."

At once, Olivia and Nick glanced up to see the spray of traditional holiday kissing greenery. The whole foyer took on an aura of unreality for Olivia. Surely, she couldn't be standing at an engagement party when she wasn't actually engaged. Surely, this crowd of people wasn't waiting for Nick to kiss her. Surely someone would snap their fingers and the guests and the mistletoe would disappear.

"I'm sorry," Nick muttered as he pulled her into his arms.

Olivia looked into Nick's gaze and saw grim determination. Lowering his head, he kissed her, and Olivia understood that she was in for the performance of her life. She wondered if she would be able to pull it off.

Nick's lips lingered as if to offer silent consolation and support. When he pulled back, he laced his fingers between hers and held tight. He shook his head. "Anna, how did you manage such a surprise?"

"I swore everyone to secrecy," she said, clearly proud of her success. She ushered Nick and Olivia into her large, elegant den decorated profusely with holiday knickknacks. "Most of the guests are from the neighborhood, but I invited a few people from your office." She waved toward Helen, her escort, Bob and Karen, as they stepped forward.

"Congratulations again!" Helen said, giving Nick and Olivia a warm hug.

"We're all still speculating on the date," Karen, the wife of Nick's boss, hinted.

Olivia felt her entire body tighten. "We're not even looking at dates until after Christmas. We're just glad we found each other again," she said, and realized she meant that last statement with all her heart.

Nick put his arm around Olivia's waist and gave her a reassuring squeeze. "That's right. We're in no rush."

Olivia met his gaze, and the connection she felt with him calmed her. During the next hour Nick didn't leave her side, and it seemed he was always either holding her hand or keeping his arm around her waist. In the back of her mind, Olivia kept reminding herself it was all part of the show, but her body and heart wanted to believe his touch meant more. The game of pretending that she and Nick were truly in love and planning to share their lives felt a little more real.

The champagne and toasts flowed with ease, raising forbidden questions. How would it be if she and Nick were really engaged? How would she feel if he loved her with all his heart? What if she truly loved him?

A seductive euphoria slid through her veins, making it easier to pretend. For the sake of the evening, Olivia decided not to fight it. As Anna brought in an array of gifts, she and Nick were separated to make way for the hostess. From the other side of the Christmas tree, she overheard some guests talking.

"She's not at all the usual kind of woman he dates," one woman said. "I always thought Nick would marry a lawyer. That way, his wife could keep up with him."

Olivia frowned.

"I always thought it would take an Ivy League type to land him," another woman said. "Did you know she didn't start college until this year?"

"Is that so?" the first woman asked. "She's not at all the usual kind of woman he dates."

"Maybe that's why he fell for her," the other woman said. "She's a novelty."

"I wonder if it will last."

It won't! Olivia wanted to tell the women even though her heart felt ripped in two. It would all be over in less than ten days. Nick would become Richmond's Bachelor of the Year again, Olivia would struggle to complete her degree, and they would go their separate ways.

Reality cut at her. This was such a farce, she thought, struggling with a desperate feeling. Surely they could leave soon.

"Time to open your gifts," Anna said, and Olivia prayed she could keep her misery to herself.

Eleven

By the time she and Nick returned to his house with gifts in tow, Olivia was numb. She wanted to turn her back on the damning sight of the gifts. They represented sincere, good wishes, and she felt anything but sincere. "I need a shower," she said, immediately heading for the stairs.

"Hold on a minute." Nick clasped his hand around her wrist. "Are you okay?"

"Just tired" she said, not turning to face him.

He tugged her backward, and her stomach took a double flip. "You don't sound okay."

"I'm fine," she said, wishing she could sound more convincing.

He turned her around. "You don't look okay."

"I thought you said I looked beautiful," she said, and managed a strained smile.

"I'm not talking about your beauty and you know it," Nick said.

Olivia felt like a house of cards. It would only take a stiff breeze and she would tumble into disarray. "You might not want to use your Warrior Commando super powers on me right now, Nick. It could get messy, and you don't like messes."

From her peripheral vision, she saw the stack of gifts and squished her eyes closed. "Oh, damn."

"What is it?" Nick demanded.

"The gifts," Olivia said. "They'll need to be returned."

"I'll handle it," he told her.

"We shouldn't have opened them," she said, her eyes filling with tears. "Everyone was so happy for us, and I felt like such a fraud."

He took her by her shoulders. "Olivia, you are not a fraud. You are the most real woman I've ever known."

"But these people care about you, Nick. I feel dishonest," she whispered.

"Hush," he said, holding her, clearly trying to soothe her distress. "Anna took us by surprise. That's why you're upset."

"Sometimes when I'm pretending to be crazy for you, I don't feel like I'm pretending," she confessed, and swallowed over the lump in her throat. "I think I might want you more than I should."

The depth of emotion in his eyes floored her. "I *know*," he told her in a rough voice, "I want you more than I should."

Then he kissed her and obliterated everything from

her consciousness except him. He was warm, and his hands and mouth were like a consuming fire burning away her pain. In his arms, the outside world fell away. Sipping at her tears, he made her feel as if she weren't all alone in her feelings.

She wanted to be the woman that fired his passion, that made him lose some of his precious control. She wanted to be the woman he trusted and turned to when he celebrated or when he mourned. She feared his possession at the same time she craved it.

"I want to make love to you. Now," he told her. "A moment didn't pass tonight when I didn't want to take you away from Anna's house so we could be alone."

His breaths came in quick bursts, and she could feel his arousal as he brushed against her. His urgency felt like gasoline, and she was already burning. Wordless, she pressed her open mouth against his and tugged at his shirt and slacks.

He unzipped her dress and pushed it down with her stockings. A second later her bra joined her other clothing on the floor. Nick immediately cupped her bottom and pulled her against him.

"Upstairs," he muttered, dragging his mouth down to her breasts. He swore. "How can it be too fast and not fast enough at the same time?"

If her vocal cords would have worked, she would have said, "The same way you can be too much, yet make me want more of you at the same time."

They climbed the stairs together, kissing and caressing each other with each step. He knew exactly where to touch her, exactly how to kiss her. Olivia was burning up. In his darkened bedroom, he took her mouth in a scorching, sexually claiming kiss that left her moaning.

"I've got to slow down," he muttered.

"No," she protested.

"Yes," he said, his nostrils flaring with each inhalation. He tugged her with him to the CD player, hit the power button, and let the slow jazz music fill the crackling air.

Pulling her flush against him, he took her mouth again and began to move.

Her heart hammering, her body clamoring for more intimacy, she struggled for her breath. "What are you doing?"

"We're dancing," he said.

"We're naked."

"I know," he said.

His chest rubbed over her breasts, tightening her nipples. His thigh slid between hers. He rocked his hard masculinity seductively where she was damp and swollen for him. Olivia inhaled deeply and drew in his scent.

She wanted to drown in all the sensations he evoked. Everything about him drew her, teased her. He was so deliciously close, yet not quite close enough. Her heart hammered against her rib cage and she lifted her mouth to his.

The brush of his tongue over hers, combined with his rhythmic intimate movements, was so erotic she could barely breathe.

"You feel so good," he told her, sliding his hands down to her bottom.

"Oh, Nick," she murmured. "I want you—" She broke off when he kissed her again.

"How do you want me, Olivia?" he asked in a voice that combined sex and silk.

At another time her need might have made her blush, but her body was on fire. "I want you—" she swallowed "—in me."

His eyes lit like twin flames as he guided her backward. The wall was cool at her back. He lifted her and she instinctively wrapped her legs around his waist.

Inch by incredible inch, he slid inside her.

Olivia gasped, tightening around his sensual invasion. His possession was so intense she struggled to keep her eyes open. She didn't want to miss a second of seeing him or feeling him.

He sucked in a deep breath and began to pump. "You're so tight, so good. I can't get enough of you."

With a mind-blowing rhythm, he filled her stroke by stroke, and Olivia wanted his words to be true. For more than just a night.

Nick didn't let her out of bed until noon the following day. For the umpteenth time, his hand snaked around her waist as she tried to crawl out of bed.

Languid from their lovemaking, she collapsed on the bed and laughed. "Food! Water!" she cried. "Bathroom!"

He pulled her against him and gave an evil-looking grin. "I'm not ready to release you."

"Then I'll die of thirst, and it will be all your fault,

and they won't name you Bachelor of the Year again.''

He shook his head and played with a strand of her hair. "You're not helping your case.''

She lowered her lids and affected a sexy pout. "Maybe this will,'' she said, and pinched him.

He jerked and scowled.

Taking full advantage, Olivia shimmied off the bed and scrambled toward the master bath.

The door slammed shut just as she reached it. Olivia saw Nick's large hand on the door at the same time she felt his other hand slide around her waist.

She sighed and gave a mock sobbing sound. "I need to get dressed. I need—''

"No, you don't.''

She turned around and leaned against the door. "I want food.''

"What a demanding woman.'' He nodded and his gaze fell over her bare body with breathtaking speed. "Okay. Go ahead and fill the Jacuzzi. I'll bring you food and drink.'' He dropped a kiss on her forehead. "I like the way you look in my bed.''

Her heart stuttered. "So, if I were machine washable, I'd be almost as good as a comforter?''

"Almost.'' He grinned over his shoulder and walked away. "Jacuzzi's almost as good as the washing machine.''

Olivia groaned and turned into the bathroom. The man could literally make her crazy. One minute she was falling under his spell, the next she wanted to slap his very nice bare rear end.

After gulping down a glassful of water, she

glanced in the mirror and swallowed a shriek. "O-migod," she murmured, combing her fingers through her mussed hair. Her eyes were bloodshot, her lips swollen from kisses, her skin pink from Nick's beard rubbing her face. She closed her eyes, hoping her image would change. She opened them and found the same sight.

"I look like a hussy," she said, then lowered her voice. "Or like I have a love hangover."

The word "love" jangled inside her like an old alarm clock. "I don't love Nick. I don't love Nick. I don't love Nick," she said, and turned away from the mirror when her eyes begged to differ.

After washing her face, she turned the jets in the hot tub on full blast to drown out the singsong rhyme that played in her head with childish glee. *Liar, liar, pants on fire.*

There were a million reasons she shouldn't love Nick. As she waited for the tub to fill, she named them. One: he didn't love her. Two: he had such a strong personality that he would overwhelm her. Three: he didn't love her. Four: she wasn't right for him. Five: he didn't love her....

She continued her list as she stepped into the tub. She was on number twenty when Nick appeared with a tray of pastries, fruit, and orange juice.

"A mermaid in my tub," Nick said, setting the tray down. "Some guys have all the luck."

Her heart melted along with the twenty reasons she couldn't love him. Olivia *knew* what she looked like. She gave a gentle smile. "You're not wearing your contacts, are you?"

He made a sexy sound that mixed a growl with a chuckle, then put his hand on her head and dunked her.

Sputtering as she lifted her head out of the water, she pushed her wet hair out of her face and glared at him. "You really know how to spoil a moment."

He brought the goblets of orange juice with him into the tub and sat beside her. "Let me see if I can make it up to you."

Accepting the glass, Olivia drank several sips and took a deep breath as he put his arm around her shoulders. "This is nice," she conceded. "Very nice."

He lifted a pastry to her lips.

She hesitated.

"Go ahead," he urged, his tone indulgent. "I don't want you fainting from hunger. I have plans for you."

A ripple of anticipation ran through her. Unable to look away, she watched him while she took a bite, then another and another. He held her glass to her lips. With each bite, with each sip, with each breath, she felt herself sinking.

"Don't be too nice to me, Nick," she warned. "I might get used to it."

He lowered his mouth to hers. "That wouldn't be so bad, would it?" He nibbled at her lips. "It's nice having you around. You make my house smile."

Her heart twisted. "I'd rather make you smile." She gulped. The secret truth slipped out of her mouth as easily as the water had poured from the jets.

"You do," he said, lifting her chin so she would

meet his gaze. "You made me smile when you were a kid with skinned knees and chopped-up bangs."

He had no idea he was touching all her private places. "I'm still lousy at snapping my fingers," she said, trying to expand the tight feeling inside her.

"Maybe you should stay around longer than thirty days," he said. "Give me a little more time, and I'll teach you."

"How would you do that?"

"Reward system. You snap your fingers," he said in a deep voice, skimming his finger down her chest, "and I'll come running."

Stop making me love you, she thought, feeling her protests and defenses slip from her grasp and helpless to stop it. "You better be careful what you offer. Snapping my fingers and having a Warrior Commando at my beck and call is pretty darn tempting."

He took her glass, returned it to the tray, and turned back to her. Lifting her hand, he took one of her fingers into his mouth.

A soft moan slipped from her throat. "What are you doing?"

"Just tempting a mermaid," he told her. "Is it working?"

"Too well," she told him. He had no idea how well.

"Practice," he said.

Olivia blinked in confusion. "Practice?"

"Snap your fingers. I'll come running."

Olivia made a lame attempt. Nick kissed her, and she was lost. Lost in love. For all her struggling to fight it, she loved Nick. She loved him for his strengths and even his flaws. The depth and strength of her love frightened her.

She could spend a lifetime trying to please this man. She could devote forever to reaching past his defenses and winning him. A dozen self-protective protests clamored through her mind. Olivia had been pushed a little too far, however, and she was impatient with fear.

She had never loved like this before, and she suspected she never would again. She kissed him for all the nights they wouldn't share. She stroked him for all the smiles she wouldn't see, all the laughter she wouldn't hear.

She felt his heart hammer against her cheek after she dragged her tongue down his chest.

"My turn for answers," he said through a groan as she lowered her hands beneath the water to his hardness. "What are you doing?" he asked as if he could sense the change in her, as if he could feel her abandon.

"Giving in to temptation," she said, urging him upward to sit on the padded side of the tub. Then she lowered her mouth to his full, hard arousal and made love to him as if there was no tomorrow, because Olivia knew she was on borrowed time.

The following morning Nick kissed Olivia and left for work. As if she were a condemned prisoner eating a final meal, Olivia allowed herself to stay in his bed for five minutes and let the memories of her time with Nick play through her mind.

The light blue color of his sheets reminded her of

his eyes, although his eyes weren't soft at all. They were bright and fierce with intelligence. She turned her face into his pillow and inhaled his musky scent. Closing her eyes, she conjured up the sound of his voice, his laughter.

Last night, she had almost convinced herself that he was as crazy for her as she was for him. Almost. The way he touched her and looked at her made it easy. But in the back of her mind, truth reared its head. A stab of pain sliced through her and she bit her lip.

She had broken all her rules, but her worst crime was that she'd fallen in love with him. Inch by inch, day by day, she'd let him take more and more of her heart. Her worst fears were realized. She'd fallen for him. All along she'd feared Nick possessed such a strong, dynamic identity that he would consume her. He had become too important to her. Thoughts of him nudged at her nearly every waking moment, even when she should be studying.

There was only one thing she could do now. Her heart felt as heavy as a cement block. Her sadness permeated her veins. She tried to tell herself she'd had plenty of warning. Nick had said he didn't like messy women, and Lord knew, she was messy. Despite their pretend engagement, Nick had made it clear he wasn't interested in romantic commitment.

The plain truth was, Olivia loved him and he didn't love her. He never would. Her stomach twisted at the ruthless truth. Sure, Nick was attracted to her, strongly attracted. If Olivia weren't careful, she would cling to that tiny bit of encouragement and spend the rest of her life trying to make him love her.

She had to leave. "No need to cry, girlfriend. You knew this day was coming," she muttered, and repeated it like a mantra.

Rising from his big bed, she pulled on a robe and put herself on automatic. She stripped the sheets, tossed them into the laundry, cleaned the dishes and went through the house gathering up her belongings. She smiled sadly at the thought that Nick might breathe a sigh of relief at having his neat home back under control. At least he wouldn't stumble over the shoes she left at the door anymore.

Sitting at the kitchen table, she wrote a note, read it, then threw it away. Her eyes burned with unshed tears. "No need to cry," she coached herself, hating the shakiness in her voice.

On impulse, she mixed some apple-cinnamon muffins and put them in the oven. While they were baking, she wrote another note, and threw it away, too. After she tossed her fourth draft, the timer went off.

Swearing in frustration, Olivia took the muffins out of the oven. A hard knot of distress crowded her chest. She didn't want to leave. Tough. She scratched out a quick note and signed it. Pulling the ring off her finger, she set it down. Friendship ring, he'd insisted. She put it on again, marveling at how right it felt on her finger. Closing her eyes, she hated her indecision. She couldn't keep it, she resolved. Olivia never wanted to take more than she left behind.

She climbed the stairs, cried in the shower, and packed her bags.

* * *

The smell of cinnamon teased Nick as soon as he walked through his front door. He smiled. Olivia had been cooking again. Automatically stepping around the area at the door where she sometimes left her shoes, he headed for the kitchen.

The room was clean and empty, and he felt a twinge of disappointment at not seeing her. "Olivia," he called, walking upstairs. Today he had decided to persuade her to extend their thirty-day engagement. He liked having her in his bed, in his life, and was unwilling to let her go.

Although neither of them was interested in commitment, there was no reason they couldn't live together, he reasoned. Fine with him to nip their social obligations in the bud to make her more comfortable with the idea. If there were deeper reasons he wanted her to stay, he pushed them aside for the more logical.

The stillness of the house nagging at him, he checked her room. It was neat, her belongings out of sight. Totally out of character. He frowned.

Her cosmetics usually decorated the top of the dresser, she often left a stack of folded clothes on the chair, and her shoes were rarely put away. Olivia had a problem with shoes, he thought. Eager to kick them off, she often left them where she dropped them.

His uneasiness grew. He stepped into the room and opened her closet door. None of her clothes hung in the closet. His heart took a strange plunge into his gut. He checked the dresser drawers and found them empty.

The realization hit him like a knockout punch.

She was gone.

A flurry of images from yesterday and last night raced through his mind. He had never felt closer to a woman. He had never felt more honest emotion from a woman than he had yesterday. Why had she left?

Stunned, he returned to the kitchen and the scent of cinnamon. He began to pace from one end of the floor to the other.

What had made her leave? What—

Nick caught sight of a sheet of paper on the table. On top of it, the ring he'd given Olivia seemed to mock him. He picked up the note and read it.

Dear Nick,
I'm very sorry, but I just can't pretend anymore.
                              Love,
                              Olivia

Twelve

Three nights later Nick took a drive down Cherry Lane and pushed the doorbell of the small ranch house belonging to the Polnecek family. If Olivia hadn't wreaked complete havoc in his life, and he had slept more than five minutes at a shot since she'd left, he might have chuckled at the memory of all the times he'd rang the Polneceks' doorbell as a kid, then run away before someone opened the door.

But he wasn't laughing or running.

The door opened at the same time the porch light flicked on. Olivia poked her head out and her eyes rounded in surprise. ''Nick, what are you doing here?''

''You still have some time left on our agreement,'' he said in a calm voice, though he was torn between hauling her off and wringing her pretty neck. The legal ramifications of either choice ran through his mind and he pulled the ring out of his pocket.

She looked at the ring and pain glinted through her eyes. Glancing over her shoulder, she stepped outside and pulled the door closed behind her. The winter night was cool, and she wrapped her arms around herself as she looked at him. "I'm sorry," she said. "I just couldn't pretend anymore. I felt like a fraud to everyone."

"Not to me," he said, fighting a dull ache at the distress in her voice.

"To you, to me," she said. "It was so confusing. First, I'm supposed to act like I love you in front of other people. Then we're lovers, but I'm not supposed to love you." She shook her head and bit her lip. "I just couldn't do it anymore."

"You were upset about other people," Nick began, trying to understand.

"It's not other people. It's me."

"Why?" he asked, his patience frayed. He swore. "You didn't act confused on Sunday."

Color rose high in her cheeks. "I know, but…"

"But what?"

She tightened her arms around herself and lifted her chin. "I know it probably doesn't make sense to you. It's not logical," she admitted. "I can't explain it."

"Try harder," Nick said, knowing he was pushing her, but needing answers. "How do you make love to me like I'm the most important thing in the world to you one day, and leave the next?"

"I told you I can't explain it," she said, wringing her hands.

"And I told you I wanted you to keep the damn ring," Nick said, feeling his control shredding.

Olivia shook her head. "I can't keep the ring. Every time I'd look at it, I would cry. I can't—"

"Cry!"

"Please keep your voice down." She took a deep breath. "This is already difficult for me. It's going to take me forever to get past—"

Confused as hell, Nick wanted to howl at the moon. "Get past what?"

He saw the first flicker of temper in her eyes.

"This is so easy for you. You can turn your emotions on and off, but I can't. You asked me to pretend to be your fiancée, to pretend to adore you, to pretend to love you. I'll tell you my problem, Mr. Warrior Commando. I wasn't pretending. I fell in love with you. How's that for messy?" she asked, her eyes turning shiny with unshed tears.

She didn't give him half a breath to respond.

"Don't worry. I know you don't love me. So show a little mercy. Just leave me alone and let me get the hell over you." She gave a laugh that sounded more like a sob. "Or I'll sic my father and brother on you."

Stunned, he felt the breeze from the door as she closed it behind her. He stared at the door for a full moment while he tried to absorb her rock-his-world confession. Her words echoed inside him like a gong.

Olivia loved him. The most incredible warmth pervaded his bloodstream, until the second thought followed like ice water. She didn't ever want to see him again.

When Nick decided to drown his sorrows, he had no idea it would turn into a Bad Boys Club reunion. He gave Ben a call, and somehow two turned into four at Mac 'n' Bob's on Main Street in Salem.

Nick looked at his grown-up comrades and shook his head. "You're all old married guys now. How did you manage to get out on Christmas Eve?"

"That's easy," Stan Michaels, who was now an orthopedic doctor, said. "The ladies are all at my house."

Ben gave a sly grin. "Giving Jenna Jean advice and support."

Nick was confused. He knew Jenna Jean was an attorney with a fierce reputation. He couldn't imagine why she would need advice. "Okay, I'll bite. Why?"

Stan's grin was so huge he looked ready to burst. "We're gonna have a baby."

Surprised, Nick stared at him. "I don't believe it. Congratulations," he said automatically, but the thought of babies brought Olivia to his mind, clawing at a raw place inside him. He quickly tried to banish it.

He looked at Joe Caruthers. "And I don't believe you're here, either. I was wondering if we would ever see anything more than pictures from you since you live in Colorado now."

"My wife kept planting the idea of expanding my franchise operation with a partner in Roanoke." Joe shrugged. "It gives me an excuse to come back here every now and then."

Ben took a long drink of beer. "Yep, the cheese stands alone, Nick. When are you going to stop being Bachelor of the Year?"

"Never," he said. Determined not to admit that he might as well be crying in his beer over a woman, he waved his hand at the waiter for another round for the table.

"Is that so?" Ben asked. "You know, my wife, Amelia, likes to read. She's a professor and she's a smart cookie."

"And she still married you," Stan said with tongue-in-cheek amazement.

Ben tossed him a sideways glance. "The next time you want mechanical advice on your car," he began in a mock-threatening voice.

"Okay, okay," Stan said, lifting his hand. "Finish what you were saying."

Ben, the owner of Roanoke's only successful foreign car dealership, grinned. "They get all the newspapers at the college. She noticed an interesting piece in the Richmond newspaper about wedding bells ringing for Nick Nolan."

Nick felt the threat of acid indigestion. "Misprint," he said. "Those society editors are always getting their facts messed up."

"The most interesting part of this," Ben continued as if Nick had said nothing, "was the name of the bride-to-be."

"Don't go there, Ben," Nick said.

"We all knew her," he added.

Nick rubbed his hand over his face and swore under his breath. "You set me up," he said.

Ben plastered an innocent expression on his face. "Hey, *you* called me."

"You ambushed me."

"My wife is a shrink," Joe interjected with a slight grin. "She would call this an intervention."

Nick groaned.

"Olivia Polnecek," Ben said in amazement. "Bully Butch's littler sister. How did you two get engaged?"

"Long story," Nick said, taking another drink of beer. "One I was hoping to forget tonight," he added darkly. "It wasn't a real engagement."

Stan cocked his head to one side in confusion. "So you weren't really involved?"

Nick's stomach started turning again. "I didn't say that." He looked at their expectant faces. "You don't want to hear this story," he told them.

Ben leaned back in his seat. "And miss the tale of how Nick got *involved* with the sister of the guy who once broke his nose?"

Three beers later Nick finished his story. "So she said she loves me and never wants to see me again." The knowledge still felt like a stake in his heart.

"Makes perfect sense to me," Stan said, rolling his eyes. "Do you want her back?"

Yes. The answer came, unequivocally, but he wouldn't say it out loud. He was still fighting the idea that he *needed* Olivia. Fighting it, and losing. "I got used to having her around. I got used to having her in my life."

"You were fine before you met her," Joe said.

Nick nodded. It was almost hard to remember life without Olivia, but he sure as hell hadn't thought anything major was missing. He hadn't laughed as much, he recalled. He hadn't felt as much. God knew, he wished he weren't feeling anything now.

"And now you're not," Joe said.

He thought about going back to the way his life had been before Olivia. The notion made him sick.

"Stick a fork in him," Ben said, apparently reading his face. "He's done. In love with Butch Polnecek's sister."

Nick frowned and shrugged. "I never believed in love. Not for me, anyway."

"I didn't, either," Joe said.

"Me neither," Ben said.

"Ditto for me," Stan said.

Nick's gut twisted again.

"Admitting is half the battle," Ben admitted. "We go down kicking and screaming."

"And come up smiling," Stan said.

"If you get her back," Joe added. "I can tell you from personal experience that winning a woman back after you've screwed up requires complete dedication. If you don't love her, if she's not as important to you as oxygen, don't bother. You don't need the hassle," Joe said as if his road to love had been a little rough.

Olivia was a messy, emotional woman, the kind Nick had always avoided. Not once during his time with her, however, had he wanted her out of his life.

Not once had he wanted less of her. He'd always wanted more.

She had the unique ability to make him feel powerful as a man and loved as a human being. Just being with her made him feel as if his world was right. He had the conviction that she would always look out for him, even if he didn't. Did he really want to give her up? His heart squeezed tight. *Could* he really give her up?

"Sometimes," Stan said, "surrender is the first step to victory."

"I love her," Nick said, and the words were so freeing he felt light-headed. "I want her."

His longtime friends looked at him in silence.

"I need a plan."

Ben laughed and lifted his beer in a toast. "That's the specialty of the Bad Boys Club."

Olivia's family had opened their gifts and just finished eating Christmas dinner when the doorbell rang. She was removing the dishes from the table while her mother and sister-in-law put the kids down for a nap.

The last few days had been difficult. She had hoped being with her family would soften the loss she felt from leaving Nick. Instead, her brother's young children made her think of the babies she might have had with Nick. The mistletoe her mother hung in the kitchen reminded her of Nick.

Futile thoughts, she realized, but she couldn't escape them. She missed him, and she was scared to death she would never truly get over him.

"Hey, Liv," Butch called. "Somebody's here to see you."

An itchy feeling of apprehension grated at the back of her neck. It wasn't Nick, she assured herself. If her threat of siccing her father and brother hadn't put him off, then she was certain her declaration of love had. She still winced when she remembered that conversation and the stunned look on his face.

"Just a minute," she said, and rinsed a china plate, then put it in the sink.

"Nick Nolan, I'll be darned," Butch said, shaking his head as Olivia rounded the corner to the den. Her stomach dipped to her knees.

"How did you meet Olivia again?"

Nick's gaze met hers, and she saw a determination that made her quiver. "Long story," he said. "Merry Christmas, Olivia."

"Merry Christmas," she uttered over the lump in her throat. In a tweed sport coat and jeans, he stood with an easy confidence that matched his clothes. He looked so good it hurt to meet his gaze. An onslaught of secret dreams she'd buried rushed through her mind. Heaven help her, she'd missed him.

Beyond her own panic, Olivia sensed her brother's discomfort. Her father's curiosity was palpable. "Nick lives in Richmond," she explained. "He's a successful attorney."

"How about that," her father said, taking Nick's measure. "I remember you were a brainy kid. So you and Olivia bumped into each other in Richmond."

"Yes," Nick said with a wry half grin. "Olivia has been living with me the last month."

Olivia's heart stopped. She stared at him. Oh, no, he hadn't said that. She hadn't heard him correctly. The combined stunned silence of her father and brother, however, had the effect of a ton of falling bricks.

Butch cleared his throat. "Did you say my sister has been living with you during the last month?"

Olivia heard the protective tone of his voice and cringed. For the most part Butch had reformed his bullying ways, but he was still overprotective in a few areas. Since Olivia's disastrous engagements, her love life was one of them.

"It's not really the way it seems," Olivia said quickly, alternating her attention between Butch and her father. Her father looked as if he needed someone to whack him on the back to get him breathing again. "I was living next door to Nick and my house caught on fire, and he actually rescued me and burned his hands, then let me stay at his house until I could find another place—"

Butch's face was turning red. He put his hands on his hips. "So you didn't try to take advantage of Liv?"

Nick searched Olivia's gaze, and her respiratory system shut down at what she thought she saw in his eyes. "I can't say I didn't take advantage of the situation."

She could tell the undertone in his voice was intended for her. Her stomach fluttered. Why was he here? What was he doing?

Her father jumped to his feet. "Why you—"

"You sonova—" Butch yelled.

"No!" Olivia cried, terrified Butch would break Nick's nose a second time.

Butch took a swing.

Nick's hand shot up, blocking the punch. "You did this about twenty years ago, Butch. You're not breaking my nose again," he said, giving him a hard glance. "I have more I need to say."

"Then maybe you'd better do your talking, son," her father huffed, his mouth moving into a puckered scowl.

Nick barely blinked. He turned to Olivia. "I want you to marry me."

The room began to spin.

Her mother and sister-in-law appeared at the doorway. Butch and her father looked totally confused.

Afraid to hope, Olivia held back. How many times had she wanted Nick's love for her to be true? She shook her head, her family fading from view. In her eyes, she could only see Nick. "I've already played the role of your fiancée. I don't—"

"I don't want you to be my fiancée, Olivia," he said, moving closer to her. "I want you to be my wife."

Her heart was beating so fast she feared she might faint. "I don't...I can't..." She couldn't collect her thoughts.

"I love you," Nick said.

"Don't say that," she said, feeling the threat of tears. "Don't say you love me unless you really mean it. Don't—"

Nick slid his hand to her cheek. "I love you, Olivia. I want us to be together all the time. I want to be your friend and your lover. I want to be your husband.''

She swallowed hard. ''I didn't think you could ever love me,'' she whispered.

''You were wrong.''

''Well, if you marry him, then it won't be a big deal if you drop out of school,'' her father interjected.

Olivia immediately stiffened. The nagging fear that Nick might overwhelm her slid inside her like poison.

''Olivia won't be dropping out of school,'' Nick said to her father, his gaze still on her. ''Olivia is an incredibly intelligent woman,'' he said as if it were an indisputable fact. ''She deserves a college education. She can succeed without me,'' he said wryly. ''But I'll do whatever I can to help her. I want to be there for her as much as she'll let me.''

In that moment her heart broke free. Everything inside her clicked together. Tears streamed down her face. Her mind almost couldn't believe that she had fallen in love with such an amazing man, and he not only loved her, he was determined to help her make her dreams come true. She could trust Nick with her soul. Her mind was having a tough time accepting it, but her heart wasn't.

The waiting in his gaze pulled at her. ''I'll marry you. But you'll have a messy life,'' she warned.

Nick took her in his arms and wiped the tears beneath her eyes. ''I wouldn't have it any other way.''

Epilogue

Three and a half years later Nick nearly burst with pride when his wife, Olivia Polnecek Nolan, graduated magna cum laude from Virginia Commonwealth University. She accepted her diploma and blew him a kiss. An hour later she lost her breakfast in the master bath.

Worried, Nick paced outside the bathroom door while her family waited downstairs. They were planning to go to a celebration lunch. Olivia's family was so proud of her they could hardly stand it. Her father kept telling strangers how his daughter was graduating with honors, and her mother was making noises about going back to school herself.

Olivia peeked out, wearing a wan smile.

"Is it excitement, or are you sick?" he asked, concerned about her pale complexion. "Do we need to get you to the doctor? You haven't seemed yourself the last week.''

She moved to the edge of the bed and pressed the washcloth to her forehead. ''It's partly excitement, but I suspect I'll be pitching my cookies more during the next few weeks.''

Nick frowned. She didn't seem troubled. He was. ''Then I'll take you to the doctor.''

She made a dismissive gesture with her hand. ''I've already been to the doctor. I was just looking for the right moment to tell you.''

''Tell me what?'' he asked in a clipped tone.

She gave him an assessing glance. ''I'm making you tense, aren't I? I'm sorry, sweetheart. There's really no reason to be tense,'' she said, then seemed to reconsider. ''Well, just a little tense,'' she amended.

''Olivia,'' he said, his patience fraying around the edges.

''Would you sit beside me, please?''

Nick took a deep breath and joined her on the bed.

Her lips tilted in a weird, feminine smile that made him nervous. ''Since we got married, I think there is something you have wanted, but you didn't want to ask me because you knew how important my education was to me. Whenever I asked you about it, you changed the subject. But every once in a while you gave me little clues. I promised you I would make your life messy, and it's about to get more messy.''

Nick saw the tears in her eyes and felt his heart clutch. He shook his head, remembering all the nights he'd bit his tongue and watched her go to sleep, all the times he'd looked with longing at his friends' children. He'd been so careful to keep it secret from Olivia, because even though the idea of having children with her promised a fulfillment he craved, *she* was most important to him. Olivia and her happiness.

His throat tightened with emotion. "I thought you couldn't read minds."

"I'm probably better with hearts."

"Oh, Lord," he said, feeling his own eyes dampen. "You're pregnant."

She nodded and came into his arms. "Yep. Looks like we'll be raising a Mighty Warrior Commando baby boy or—"

"A Mighty Warrior Commando baby girl," he said. "Just like her mother." He pulled back slightly to look into her eyes, shining with love. "I never knew messy could be so good."

* * * * * *

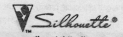

Take 2 bestselling love stories FREE

Plus get a FREE surprise gift!

Special Limited-Time Offer

Mail to Sihouette Reader Service™

P.O. Box 609
Fort Erie, Ontario
L2A 5X3

YES! Please send me 2 free Silhouette Desire® novels and my free surprise gift. Then send me 6 brand-new novels every month, which I will receive months before they appear in bookstores. Bill me at the low price of $3.49 each plus 25¢ delivery and GST*. That's the complete price, and a saving of over 10% off the cover prices—quite a bargain! I understand that accepting the books and gift places me under no obligation ever to buy any books. I can always return a shipment and cancel at any time. Even if I never buy another book from Silhouette, the 2 free books and the surprise gift are mine to keep forever.

326 SEN CH7V

Name _____ (PLEASE PRINT)

Address _____ Apt. No. _____

City _____ Province _____ Postal Code _____

This offer is limited to one order per household and not valid to present Silhouette Desire® subscribers. *Terms and prices are subject to change without notice. Canadian residents will be charged applicable provincial taxes and GST.

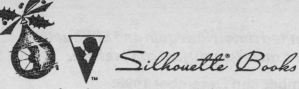

For a limited time, Harlequin and Silhouette have an offer you just can't refuse.

In November and December 1998:

BUY **ANY** TWO HARLEQUIN
OR SILHOUETTE BOOKS and
SAVE $10.00
off future purchases

OR BUY ANY THREE HARLEQUIN OR SILHOUETTE BOOKS
AND **SAVE $20.00** OFF FUTURE PURCHASES!

(each coupon is good for $1.00 off the purchase of two
Harlequin or Silhouette books)

···

JUST BUY 2 HARLEQUIN OR SILHOUETTE BOOKS, SEND US YOUR
NAME, ADDRESS AND 2 PROOFS OF PURCHASE (CASH REGISTER
RECEIPTS) AND HARLEQUIN WILL SEND YOU A COUPON BOOKLET
WORTH **$10.00 OFF** FUTURE PURCHASES OF HARLEQUIN OR
SILHOUETTE BOOKS IN 1999. SEND US 3 PROOFS OF PURCHASE AND
WE WILL SEND YOU 2 COUPON BOOKLETS WITH A TOTAL SAVING OF
$20.00. (ALLOW 4-6 WEEKS DELIVERY) OFFER EXPIRES
DECEMBER 31, 1998.

···

I accept your offer! Please send me a coupon booklet(s), to:

NAME: _____

ADDRESS: _____

CITY: _____ STATE/PROV.: _____ POSTAL/ZIP CODE: _____

Send your name and address, along with your cash register
receipts for proofs of purchase, to:

In the U.S.	In Canada
Harlequin Books	Harlequin Books
P.O. Box 9057	P.O. Box 622
Buffalo, NY	Fort Erie, Ontario
14269	L2A 5X3

PHQ4982